A Corpse for Christmas

Mrs. Lillywhite Investigates

Book Twelve

Emily Queen

Willow Hill
BOOKS

CONTENTS

British Terms

Barmy - a crazy idea

Block of flats - apartment building

Bloody - an intensifying mild expletive (swear word)

Bollocks - dismay or disbelief

Car park - parking lot

Cheeky - endearingly rude or disrespectful

Chinwag - a gossip session

Chuffed - to be very pleased or happy about something

Cracking - good or excellent; to get started doing something

Cuppa - cup of (usually tea)

Daft - a bit stupid or silly

Diamante – rhinestone

Dodgy - questionable or suspicious

Dolt - a fool

Fancy - a verb expressing desire ("do you fancy some dinner?")

Footway – sidewalk

Fringe (hair) – bangs

Gobsmacked - shocked

Holiday - vacation

Jumble sale - yard/lawn/garage sale

Loo - the toilet

Lorry - truck

Match - game

Pinch - to steal

Solicitor – lawyer

Stodgy -
Sweets - candy
To nick/to get nicked - to steal/to be arrested for a crime
Trollop - a loose woman; a woman with low morals
(derogatory)
Underground - subway

~Find more British English terms on my website~

A Corpse for Christmas

ONE

A shiver raced up Rosemary Lillywhite's spine as she leaned back against the cold porcelain sink and felt the press of its icy surface through her silk blouse. She had been hiding in the upstairs powder room of her townhouse for a few long minutes already, seeking refuge from her mother's invasive questions and relentless meddling. Through the walls, Evelyn's muffled voice instructed Rosemary's ever-patient butler, Wadsworth, on the proper way to set the table for dinner.

"Mrs. Woolridge, I assure you, the silverware will be positioned according to your exact specifications." Wadsworth's calm voice floated up the stairs.

"Very well, Wadsworth," Evelyn replied curtly as if she suspected he'd really meant her *exacting* specifications.

Rosemary rolled her eyes at the exchange. Despite having been in her home for less than an hour, Evelyn had already alienated the staff in addition to inquiring—twice—about whether Rosemary was considering becoming engaged to Max Whittington, the Chief Inspector of the London police. While she was quite fond of Max, the constant probing made her feel like a specimen pinned under a microscope, particularly given how mercurial her mother had been regarding the relationship thus far.

It wasn't that Evelyn wholly disapproved of Max. How could she when he was practically flawless? Handsome, intelligent, upright, respectful—not to mention, had worked dili-gently to clear her son's name when he was falsely accused of murder. As far as Rosemary could tell, the only item her mother could possibly add to Max's con tally was his status as a working-class man.

The one thing Rosemary couldn't give a lick about.

A man like Max, who earned his living rather than being born into wealth, provided a comforting type of security, one different from the kind her mother prized. Not that Evelyn hadn't changed her tune before, even singing Max's praises on at least one occasion, but it was hard to keep up, and Rosemary had grown weary of the task.

With a wistful sigh, she let herself fantasize about how much easier life would be if she could politely decline her moth-er's visits.

Unfortunately, Evelyn Woolridge wasn't so easily dissuaded.

Roused from her thoughts by a sharp rap on the brass door knocker, Rosemary reached the landing just in time to see her dearest friend and sister-in-law, Vera, step over the threshold with an air of practiced grace. For all of Evelyn's perfectionism, the spunky actress brought a refreshing dose of unpredictability to the family, and Rosemary felt her spirits lift immediately.

"Vera, darling," Evelyn exclaimed, the corners of her blue-grey eyes crinkling into a smile that softened her otherwise forbidding appearance. "Don't you look lovely today? And what a stunning coat!"

The garment, a tailored affair in deep emerald, slipped into the butler's waiting arms along with a matching hat adorned with a tasteful plume. "Thank you, Wads, darling," Vera said affectionately before turning to Evelyn.

"Isn't it exquisite? I just got it from Harrods." Vera's smile was as bright as her words. She shook out her short crop of coal-black hair as if shrugging off the late afternoon chill and enveloped Evelyn in a warm embrace. To Rosemary's relief, the fragile detente between mother and daughter-in-law appeared to be holding fast.

"Harrods, of course!" Evelyn replied, her voice laced with approval. "We'll have to stop there tomorrow during our shopping excursion."

"Mother, honestly, I doubt so much as a slip of paper will fit into the boot alongside what you arrived here with. How ever will you get it all back to Pardington?" Rosemary's eyes twinkled as they met Wadsworth's. Always the consummate professional, his expression never wavered.

Neither had it budged an inch during the unloading of Evelyn's cases, though Rosemary had noticed the flush of crimson he couldn't keep from coloring his cheeks. Wadsworth wasn't a young man, and she hoped her mother hadn't been working him too hard. Aside from a weekly card game, he hardly ever asked for personal time and, in fact, had only agreed to take a Christmas holiday at Rosemary's resolute insistence.

"Oh, dear," Evelyn sighed, a hint of exasperation coloring her tone. "You're worse than your father sometimes. I'll simply have everything shipped directly, won't I? Harrods is quite competent, I assure you."

Never having been afflicted with buyer's remorse, Vera nodded sagely in agreement, but Rosemary ignored her.

"Regardless, bringing half the contents of your wardrobe does seem a bit excessive for such a brief visit."

"That's not nearly half my wardrobe, darling," Evelyn replied crisply. "And as I always say, it's best to be prepared for whatever occasion might arise."

Rosemary's lips curved with gentle mirth. "You two are beginning to sound alike."

Vera laughed, quite used to being ribbed about her penchant for luxury. "Mock us if you must," she said with a wink. "You're in good company. Frederick has been trying to cure me of it for ages."

"Frederick can try all he likes," Evelyn replied dryly, "however—"

"—a leopard never changes its spots," Rosemary finished another of her mother's well-worn phrases. Laughter trailing behind, she led the way to the parlor, where a fire crackled cheerily in the hearth.

Before long, the tinkle of glass and the whisper of wheels on the carpet announced Wadsworth's arrival with the drinks trolley. Rosemary waved him away, selected a crystal decanter, and, with a practiced hand, poured rich amber liquid into three glasses. The scent of aged brandy mingled pleasantly with the lingering aroma of beeswax polish.

"Here we are," she announced, handing each woman a glass. "A little fortification against the evening chill."

"Well, then, this is quite cozy," Evelyn observed, settling onto an embroidered settee with a satisfied sigh.

"Thank you," Rosemary replied, mildly pleased despite her insistence that her mother's opinion held no weight in her decorating choices, and added innocently, "Although I must say, now that the renovations are complete, Freddie and Vera's new home boasts much more spacious rooms. The guest suite is particularly charming. A shame not to take advantage of it during your stay."

"Oh, you know your father," Evelyn said, waving a dismissive hand. "Cecil is a creature of habit. He's accustomed to staying here when we're in town. It would only confuse him to change the routine now." She took a slow sip of brandy, but her eyes remained glued to the drapes.

Rosemary arched an eyebrow. "Are you certain it isn't because Frederick and Vera don't employ a full staff at their new home?"

Evelyn's lips pursed slightly, a telltale sign that Rosemary had struck a nerve. But before she could respond, a soft pattering of paws heralded the arrival of Dash, Rosemary's vivacious German Spitz. With a joyful bark, he bounded across the room and leaped onto Evelyn's lap, tail wagging furiously.

"See, Mother? Even Dash knows you prefer the full domestic ensemble," Rosemary teased, enjoying the sight of her mother's stoic composure breaking into a reluctant smile under the little dog's enthusiastic affection.

"We both know a household runs more smoothly with a full staff," Evelyn said with a pointed stare towards the door, where Wadsworth stood discreetly. "It's naught but a matter of time before Frederick and Vera accept the fact themselves."

Vera laughed and aimed a cheeky wink at the butler. "Given that Rosemary has already monopolized the most impeccable services available, what hope did Frederick and I have? We're rather doomed to inefficiency, I'm afraid." Despite his well-known soft spot for Vera's bold disposition, Rosemary noticed that Wadsworth's responding smile didn't quite reach his eyes.

"I'm perfectly capable of managing without a battalion of servants, you know," Evelyn chided, stroking Dash's fluffy head. "I quite enjoy a bit of rustic charm now and then."

"Independence does have its charms, Mrs. Woolridge," Vera replied lightly, "though I'm afraid I find the term rustic somewhat inaccurate. Nevertheless, Frederick and I take great delight in our little domestic adventures. He's organized his wardrobe down to the cuff links, and you ought to see how he's decorated his study," she added with a hint of pride.

Unmoved, Evelyn merely smiled and abruptly changed the subject. "We've more important things to discuss, don't we?"

"Such as?" Rosemary asked, genuinely curious as to what her mother deemed more pressing than meddling in her children's lives, no matter how inconsequential the topic.

"Tomorrow's factory tour, of course," Evelyn declared, her voice regaining its authoritative edge. "The American expansion is a significant opportunity for Woolridge & Sons, and we cannot afford any missteps. We must all put our best faces forward."

Rosemary's tone sharpened. "Rest assured, Mother, we'll all be on our best behavior until told otherwise. All attempts to embarrass the family will be postponed until after the new year."

"Your sarcasm is unbecoming, Rosemary," Evelyn scolded, her gaze as unwavering as a hawk's. "I expect each of you to conduct yourselves appropriately during the tour. We must show the potential investors that Woolridge & Sons is a company shaped by good old-fashioned family values."

Rosemary resisted the urge to roll her eyes, knowing that even the subtlest expression wouldn't escape her mother's scrutiny. Instead, she opted for a more diplomatic approach and pasted on a serene smile. "Yes, Mother. Of course."

Evelyn scrutinized her daughter's face briefly but seemed satisfied enough to let the matter drop. She turned her attention back to Wadsworth, who was dutifully tending to the drinks, and began explaining how to mix a gimlet precisely to her liking.

"Of course, Mrs. Woolridge, as you wish."

Rosemary exchanged a small, conspiratorial smile with Vera

just as the lively jingle of the doorbell announced Cecil and Frederick's arrival. As the door swung open, father and son entered with the air of those bearing good tidings, their neckties adorned with sprightly holly patterns that caught the light with each step.

"Mother!" Frederick exclaimed warmly, depositing an affectionate kiss on her cheek. "I dare say you look positively radiant this evening."

Cecil followed suit, pulling Evelyn into an embrace that thawed her usual reserve. "That description doesn't do you justice, dear."

For a fleeting moment, Evelyn's face lit with unguarded fondness. "Always the charmer."

Rosemary observed the scene from her vantage point near the drinks trolley, a small smile tugging at her lips. Watching her stern mother soften under her husband's charm was like witnessing frost melt under the warmth of the morning sun and had a similar effect on her own mood.

The conversation turned to their upcoming family commitments, each detail scheduled down to the minute, as Evelyn always insisted. Yet despite the regimented nature of her mother's plans, Rosemary couldn't help but feel a flicker of anticipation for the festive days ahead.

"We'll all go to Clerkenwell for the factory tour first thing tomorrow," Evelyn explained. "And I've taken the liberty of making dinner reservations for the family at Kettner's. Have you spoken to your sister?"

"Yes. Stella rang earlier to say she'll be on the first train from Oxford tomorrow morning. Leonard still has a few classes to teach before the official end of term, and she thought it best to leave the children with the nanny rather than drag them all around London. She said little Nelly put up quite a fuss and would only settle once reassured he was still going to visit his grandparents for Christmas."

Evelyn smiled at the mention of her grandson and nodded. "I anticipated that might be the case, so I only reserved a table for eight."

"Eight?" Frederick asked, looking around the room with a puzzled expression.

"Yes, eight. The five of us," she said, holding up a finger for each name, "Stella, and then, I thought it might be nice to invite Uncle Henry and your cousin Miranda. After all, Henry deserves to celebrate as much as anyone."

Cecil beamed at his wife. "Indeed. Our finances would be an utter disaster without my brother's guiding hand. He'll be chuffed, I'm sure, to have been included. However, I won't hazard a guess as to Miranda's availability."

"If she declines, perhaps we could invite Max," Rosemary suggested, mildly annoyed her mother hadn't thought to reserve a seat for the man she'd been pestering her daughter to marry.

"I'm sorry, dear," Evelyn replied airily, "I wasn't aware that his intention to join us in Pardington over Christmas meant he was also to be included in all other family gatherings."

"Max is coming to Pardington after all?" Vera inquired, her voice laced with curiosity as she settled back into the armchair near the fire, hands wrapped around a still-full brandy glass.

"Yes," Rosemary brightened. "His mother's hip has improved significantly, and she decided to join her friends for a holiday in the tropics. Who would have thought it?"

"Speaking of holiday travels," Vera added, leaning back with a conspiratorial grin, "Mother's found herself a new beau. They're also basking in some sun-drenched locale while we brave the London chill." She let out a warm laugh, the sound light and musical against the crackling fire. "He's quite the character from what I hear—flashy, charming. Just Mother's style."

"A holiday fling, perhaps? Or something more serious?" Frederick teased, his expression sly as he swirled the port in his glass, watching the rich liquid catch the firelight.

"Oh please," Vera rolled her eyes playfully, her laughter bubbling. "Mother's not one for flings anymore."

"Well, she certainly deserves some happiness after all these years," Evelyn interjected, her usual cool demeanor softening at the mention of her most coveted friend. "I do hope this new gentleman treats her well."

"He'd better," Rosemary said, her tone stern but her eyes twinkling with amusement as she glanced at Vera. "Or he'll have you to contend with, I suppose."

Before Vera could reply, the door creaked open, and Max appeared.

"Speak of the devil." Frederick raised his glass.

"Evening, everyone." Max nodded respectfully towards the Woolridges before turning his focus on Rosemary. "I apologize for my tardiness. I hope I haven't missed too much."

"Only a discussion of our holiday plans," she replied, brightening as he sat beside her. "And how glad we are that you'll join us this year."

Max's mouth turned into a wider grin than the one he habitually wore, but he didn't have time to reply before Frederick pressed a glass into his hand and said, "Wait until you see Woolridge House all done up in Christmas garb. It's a sight to behold, especially the tree."

"The tallest one Father can get his hands on," Rosemary added, "and then we all decorate it together."

"Ah, yes," Cecil chuckled, leaning back into his armchair.

"Little Nelly is always so excited to participate, even though half of the ornaments end up clustered around the bottom branches. I remember when Frederick and Lionel were young lads—they'd do the very same thing, piling everything within reach of their chubby little arms."

"Father, please," Frederick groaned, rolling his eyes as he sipped his drink. "You're worse than Mother."

"Sounds like quite the festive gathering," Max remarked, his voice tinged with genuine cheer as he met Rosemary's gaze with another of his disarming smiles. She felt her heart flutter but refrained from gazing at him adoringly within view of her mother.

"Indeed," Cecil agreed, his expression softening as he surveyed his family, pride evident in his eyes. "I can hardly wait." With a small flourish, he rose from his armchair, balancing a glass of port in one hand. He made his way to Evelyn and, in a tender, intimate gesture, adjusted the delicate pearl necklace resting at her throat.

"Ah, my little Pavlova," he murmured, just loud enough for the room to hear. A flush of color crept into Evelyn's cheeks, and she allowed herself a smile that could only be described as radiant.

"Really, Cecil!" Evelyn scolded lightly, but her protest lacked any real bite. "Such nonsense." Yet, the twinkle in her eye spoke of her delight. For a moment, she looked almost like a young girl again, the graying strands of hair around her face the same golden shade as Rosemary's in the glow of the firelight.

The room fell silent, everyone observing their quiet affection until Max cleared his throat and rose, lifting his wine glass in a modest toast. "I'd like to say Merry Christmas to you all and thank you for welcoming me into your holiday traditions. It means a great deal."

Cecil nodded and raised his glass, but it was Evelyn who responded smoothly, "Of course, Max. We're more than happy to have you as part of the family." Her gaze flicked meaningfully to Rosemary.

The underlying message was quite clear, and Rosemary suppressed a sigh, feeling the familiar weight of her mother's expectations settle on her shoulders. Evelyn's constant nudging was like a pebble in her shoe, never quite painful enough to confront but ever-present.

Fortunately, her father deftly redirected the conversation, launching into an animated description of the annual Woolridge & Sons holiday benefit. "Every year, the neighborhood children gather in the factory courtyard and enjoy a visit from jolly old Santa Claus himself," Cecil explained, "and each child leaves with a wrapped gift."

It was no wonder where Frederick got his charm, Rosemary thought as she watched her father, his enthusiasm belying his usual businesslike demeanor.

Suitably impressed, Max beamed. "A worthwhile endeavor, if I've ever heard one."

"Nothing warms the heart quite like giving back," Cecil agreed. "Especially during the holiday season."

The heavenly scent of freshly baked pastry filled the room as the cook, Gladys, entered carrying a tray laden with mince pies.

"Fresh from the oven," she declared proudly, her cheeks flushed from the kitchen's warmth. "I couldn't help but overhear your discussion about the charity event, and I wanted to thank you. I'm from Clerkenwell, you know, and your generosity means a lot to those families. For some, those gifts will be the only ones beneath the tree on Christmas morning."

Evelyn's brow furrowed as she considered Gladys's statement.

"It's our pleasure," Cecil said humbly, waving off the praise.

"We must all do our part," Evelyn agreed, her tone tempered by a rare moment of humility Rosemary suspected had something to do with the fact that while she wrote a generous check every year, she had never actually attended the company's annual charity event. "It is only right."

After Gladys returned to the kitchen, Frederick leaned forward, his already boyish grin brightening further. "It's also good for business. Two birds, one stone. Charles Harrington, who will head our new American division, has even agreed to don the Santa suit this year in Uncle Henry's stead."

"That's probably for the best. Uncle Henry could do with taking a year off," Rosemary mused aloud, picturing the stately executive struggling with the costume the year before. "He grumbled about it last year from start to finish, if memory serves."

"That is," Cecil said, "until the children arrived. He's always much better with children than he is with adults."

Frederick snorted. "A fact I'm certain our investors will attest to. It's good we didn't leave him in charge of bolstering the charity coffers."

"No, certainly not," Cecil replied, eyes twinkling. "Your bit of trickery was all we needed for that. We've secured more donations this year than ever before. The checks have been pouring into the office all month."

"Whatever do you mean?" Vera asked, eying her husband curiously.

Frederick took his time answering. "Oh, just a bit of artful manipulation, if you will. I simply mention the event in passing, never asking for donations directly. People are much more generous when they believe the act of giving was entirely their own idea."

"My brother, the strategist," Rosemary remarked with a wry chuckle, imagining guests reaching for their wallets, moved by the festive spirit and Frederick's subtle persuasion.

"These mince pies are delicious," Cecil remarked around a mouthful of pastry, earning a reproachful glance from Evelyn, who had, for a long moment, been staring contemplatively at the air just above his head. "We should add them to our holiday menu."

"The Christmas menu has been planned out for months, darling."

"I'm glad you're enjoying them, Father," Rosemary replied without acknowledging her mother's comment. "I'll pass the compliment along to Gladys."

Frederick's expression turned mischievous as he settled back into the plush settee, cradling his glass in one hand. "Mother, I must say, it's quite the clever strategy to avoid our humble abode," he teased. "One might think you're sparing yourself the horror of dealing with our nonexistent servants."

Posed as a challenge, Frederick's comment lingered in the air. Evelyn's composure faltered ever so slightly, her lips pursing in a display of annoyance rarely directed towards her precious son.

Vera chuckled softly, her fingers curling around Frederick's in a subtle gesture of support. "It's a good thing we manage well enough on our own, isn't it, Freddie?"

"We do," Frederick agreed, his gaze on Vera softening. "And quite comfortably, I might add."

Evelyn leveled her gaze on her son. "Frederick, dear, how fortunate Vera is to have married a man who excels at making himself comfortable."

Two

The following afternoon, crisp December air nipped at Rosemary's cheeks as she and Vera followed Evelyn into the Woolridge & Sons company offices. Veteran staff still fondly referred to the impressive structure as the "new" building, even though it had been several years since the company had grown enough to necessitate moving the administrative portion away from the factory space.

Nestled in the heart of Bloomsbury, the building's understated elegance was a testament to Cecil's shrewd business acumen. After being stripped bare for refurbishment by the previous owner before financial woes forced it into auction, Cecil had acquired the building for hardly more than a whisper and a song.

"It's coming along rather nicely, isn't it?" Vera murmured as they passed through the wide-open doors into the heart of the company.

"Quite," Rosemary wholeheartedly agreed. Her father's decision to raise the ceilings gave the place an airier feel than its utilitarian exterior suggested and allowed in more light—and to her artist's eye, more light was always better than less.

Rosemary admired both her father's tenacity and his subsequent restraint. Where other businessmen might have prioritized a set of posh offices, Cecil had remained patient, slowly shaping the interior into one both innovative and inviting. Except for one section, anyway.

The reception area was a tidy but undeniably cramped affair, with the secretary's desk tucked into a wooden booth with glass partitions on three sides, giving her a semblance of privacy while still leaving her visible to anyone entering the office. Inside the booth, the space was a cluttered amalgamation of essential equipment: the switchboard with its tangle of cords and blinking lights, a stack of files teetering precariously on the edge of the desk, and an overflowing inkwell with smudged pens scattered around.

To make matters worse, several large boxes had been stacked behind the desk, the booth's tight quarters lending it the distinct feeling of being wedged inside a stationery cupboard.

Cecil gestured towards the switchboard as Rosemary entered, his tone clipped but cheerful. "We've just installed this newfangled telephone system—direct lines and all. That one," he added, pointing to a prominent black wire running from the board, "connects straight to the factory. It's supposed to save us from sending messengers up and down Clerkenwell, but between you and me, I'm not convinced it's worth the bother yet. Lois is barely managing as it is."

As the procession continued, Rosemary noticed Vera's familiar interaction with the staff. She seemed to know everyone by name, sharing smiles and pleasantries as they passed. But then, it didn't come as much of a surprise, considering Vera had always been the more outgoing of the pair.

"Evelyn, ladies! Welcome," a familiar voice broke her momentary reverie. Henry Woolridge, Cecil's older brother, looked every bit as much a fixture in the office as the mahogany desks. His warm smile and bright eyes contrasted with the slight sadness lingering around him. As usual, he appeared somewhat disheveled, tie slightly askew, one lock of gray hair sticking up on end. A smudge of ink on his cheek suggested he'd been poring over reports again, and absentmindedly rubbed his face.

"Uncle Henry!" Rosemary smiled, offering a hand, which he shook heartily before similarly greeting Vera.

Beside Henry stood his daughter, Miranda, who posed a stark contrast to her father's unruly appearance. She wore a tailored suit in a muted color, every button and seam impeccable, fair hair pulled back into a neat chignon.

Next to her, Rosemary felt positively bohemian even if she had remained resolute against Vera suggestion to cut her hair into a fashionable bob. Still, with Miranda's coloring being so similar, Rosemary found herself tempted to let Vera have her way, if for no other reason than to look less like Miranda.

First cousins born during the same summer, she and Rosemary ought to have been bosom buddies, but that had never been the case. Their kinship barely extended beyond formal pleasantries for reasons that continued to vex Rosemary. Ever eager for approval, Miranda chose to sip tea with or learn proper etiquette from Aunt Evelyn rather than scamper through hedgerows or secret passages with the rest of the children.

"Are you excited about the American expansion?" Rosemary asked, hoping for a spark of warmth only to be met with an ice-blue stare that, while composed and expressionless, still struck her as mildly disdainful.

When Miranda didn't reply, her attention captured by a clerk hurrying past with an armload of fabric samples, Henry glanced at her with a mixture of affection and mild exasperation. "Yes, yes, of course, it's all quite thrilling, isn't it?" he answered in her stead, but his voice lacked enthusiasm. "Between you and me, I'll be happy when the whole project is out of my hands so I can stop burning the midnight oil."

"It sounds as though Charles Harrington will do a bang-up job running the New York division," Vera commented, briefly bringing Miranda's attention back to the conversation. "According to Frederick, anyway. He says business is excellent."

"Excellent, yes," Miranda replied vaguely, "Father says they've already secured orders enough to keep the new machines running until Easter."

"Actually, darling, it's until August," Henry explained proudly. "However, those are preliminary estimates, not secured orders."

"Oh, of course, August," she replied with a feigned interest so thin it might tear at a touch. Miranda's presence was ostensibly to show family unity, but Rosemary couldn't help but notice the vacant expression that settled on her face whenever discussions turned to looms and linens. She watched as Henry offered quiet corrections to her misguided statements, his voice carrying no rancor, only the enduring patience of a father perennially smoothing the creases from his daughter's life.

Dubbed "good old Henry" by his brother, some mistook her uncle's mild manner for timidity. Rosemary, however, considered him very much like a duck—appearing to glide serenely on top of the water while paddling like crazy beneath the surface.

This had never been more evident than the day his wife—Miranda's mother—had vanished without a trace. The news sent ripples through the Woolridge family. Whispers behind closed drawing-room doors and the sympathetic clucks of tongues feasting on the scandal like Sunday roast while Henry seemed unaffected. Still, from then on, acting out of guilt or perhaps fear, he had lavished fineries and affection upon Miranda—an obvious attempt to fill the void left by a woman whose absence was as palpable as the cold side of a once-warm bed.

And Miranda, who now turned her attention towards Evelyn with a smile more genuine than any she'd ever spared for Rosemary, had always appeared caught in the tide between seeking approval and safeguarding her heart. After Andrew's passing, something in her had shifted, softening like wax under the warmth of shared grief. Losing a husband wasn't the same as losing a mother, but the pain had brought the cousins closer. For a while at least, but now, with Miranda hardly sparing her a glance, it was beginning to feel like old times.

Before she could give her cousin's demeanor much more thought, the new secretary—Lois, she remembered from her father's comment earlier—caught Rosemary's attention as the poor girl struggled to manage a cascade of papers determined to escape her grasp. Each slip fluttered like a leaf on the wind, leading the unfortunate young woman on a clumsy ballet through the busy office.

"Pardon me, excuse me," Lois mumbled, cheeks flushed with embarrassment as she dodged around bustling workers and wove her way through rows of desks to the disjointed tune of a Christmas carol rendered unidentifiable by the relentless cacophony of clacking typewriter keys.

Observing the commotion from a safe distance, Evelyn pressed her lips into a thin line of restrained disapproval, making it clear she found the young woman's fluster exasperating, yet her impeccable manners prevented an outward show of critique. This was her husband's domain, after all.

"Lois, dear, perhaps it's best to sort papers at your desk," she suggested lightly.

"Thank you, Mrs. Woolridge," Lois replied, voice trembling, eyes wide with the panic of a gazelle who had strayed too close to a lion's den.

As Rosemary moved to offer assistance, a burst of laughter echoed from above. All heads turned towards the upper balcony where a man—Charles Harrington, Rosemary surmised—made his entrance, the plush red fabric of a Santa Claus suit hugging his frame with jovial pomp. A fluffy cloud of white faux beard bobbed up and down as he descended the stairs with a boisterous "Ho ho ho and Merry Christmas!" filling the room with delight.

The office erupted in cheers and bright smiles. Even the sternest of accountants couldn't resist the infectious spirit Mr. Harrington conjured with his hearty chuckles and twinkling eyes.

"Hello, Mrs. Woolridge and Mrs. Woolridge junior," he joked, greeting Evelyn and Vera in turn. "You're both looking lovely as always. And you must be the famous Rosemary I've heard so much about."

"Pleased to meet you, Mr. Harrington," she replied politely.

"Charles, please," he said with a smile before his eyes landed on Miranda. She offered no more acknowledgment than a curt nod, but still, he asked, "How are you today? I hope all is well." When her indifferent expression remained unchanged, he didn't miss a beat, saying, "Well, it's been a pleasure, ladies," before sauntering off.

Rosemary watched as he exchanged jovial quips with the milling staff until he caught sight of Lois, whose cheeks were flushed with embarrassment as she chased after the fluttering sea of papers.

"Let me lend a hand," Charles said, stooping to retrieve a stray sheet that had pirouetted away. As he passed it back to her, their fingers brushed momentarily, and Lois offered a grateful smile that softened the hard lines of worry around her eyes.

"Thank you, Mr. Harrington. I'm afraid it's just one of those days." Her voice was slightly breathy and tinged with chagrin.

"Everyone has them," Charles assured her with a wink, his tone warm enough to melt the chill of December outside. Rosemary admired how he navigated the space with an easy charm that felt rare and essential in the stiff-collared business world. Her father carried a share of it, and Frederick had it to the nth degree, so she wasn't surprised to discover that the man they'd chosen to represent them in the States was cut from the same cloth.

Everyone's attention snapped to the main entrance when the door swung open to reveal a figure clad in a stylish winter dress and matching cloak—Lady Beatrice Foxworthy, a well-known socialite, philanthropist, and dear old family friend.

"Good afternoon, all!" Lady Foxworthy's voice rang out brightly, the feather in her hat bobbing jauntily as she made her way inside. Rosemary noticed how Henry's typically composed expression softened for just an instant, betraying the faintest flicker of emotion—as well as how her mother greeted her friend with a smile that, while genuine, stopped just short of her eyes.

"Beatrice, how lovely to see you," Evelyn greeted smoothly, kissing each of Lady Foxworthy's cheeks in turn.

"Evelyn, girls, you all look positively radiant," Lady Foxworthy gushed. "Oh, and Miranda, what did I tell you? That new hairstyle is quite fetching on you, isn't it?"

While Miranda patted her hair with a pleased smile, Cecil deftly sidestepped the greetings with a polite nod and strode to the center of the office. Without a word, his presence commanded attention, and the chatter died down as all eyes turned towards him.

"May I have your attention, please," Cecil began, "First and foremost, I want to express my deepest gratitude to each and every one of you. Your hard work, dedication, and unwavering commitment to Woolridge & Sons have been the driving force behind our success."

"As you all know, the upcoming factory tour is paramount. It's a chance for us to showcase the innovation, craftsmanship, and heart that goes into every yard of fabric we produce. We have the opportunity to secure the confidence of our investors and pave the way for our American expansion."

Cecil's eyes sparkled with excitement as he spoke of the future, his enthusiasm infectious. "However," he continued, his tone growing more serious, "I want to make one thing abundantly clear. No matter the tour's outcome or the challenges we may face, you—our employees—will always be our priority. In just a couple of days, we'll be closing for the holidays," Cecil went on, his voice warm with sincerity. "And when you receive your pay, you'll find something extra inside—a token of our appreciation for all you do."

The office erupted in a chorus of cheers and applause. Rosemary felt a swell of pride for her father, a man who understood that a company's true strength lay not in its balance sheets but in the hearts and minds of those who dedicated their lives to its success.

When the commotion had died down, Lady Foxworthy's hands fluttered in an exaggerated gesture only a woman of her breeding could manage without seeming entirely absurd. "A factory tour? My dear Evelyn, I thought today was the children's benefit!"

"Ah, I suspect that would be Lois's doing," Evelyn replied,

her smile as restrained as ever. "But since you're here, do join us for the tour. Several affluent investors are in attendance, and your presence would certainly add...flair."

Lady Foxworthy's laugh rang out above the din. "It usually does."

Rosemary observed the exchange curiously, noting the contrast between her mother's composed demeanor and Lady Foxworthy's exuberant flair. It was like watching a swan glide among a flamboyance of flamingos.

Mother certainly chooses the most colorful friends, Rosemary mused inwardly, recalling evenings with Lorraine Blackburn's dramatic stories and Cecily DeVant's impassioned debates. Evelyn's drawing room had often buzzed with energy while she remained the calm eye of the storm.

Perhaps she finds a vicarious thrill in their adventures, Rosemary considered with a wry smile before thinking better of it. Her mother merely enjoyed being the steady presence amidst her friends' exuberance. All the easier to say I told you so the moment things didn't go their way.

"I look forward to seeing what Woolridge & Sons has in store," Lady Foxworthy said, her gaze lingering on Henry long enough to summon a faint blush before turning away.

Frederick leaned close to Rosemary, whispering with a conspiratorial grin, "It's the thrill of the chase, Rosie. Our dear uncle is smitten, and the lady is none the wiser."

"That's where you're wrong, Freddie," she lobbed back. "A lady always knows."

"Excuse me, Mr. Woolridge," Lois said, timidly approaching Cecil, "it's that chap again—Albert Gibbs—he insists on speaking with you." Her hands clutched a handful of pink telephone message slips as she struggled to maintain her composure under the scrutiny of his gaze.

Cecil cocked his head, the gears of memory turning. "Lois, my dear, there must be some confusion. Albert Gibbs hasn't worked here for years. Are you certain it was him?"

"Perfectly certain, sir. He mentioned something about the new fabric shipment," Lois replied, her fingers tightening around the papers as if they might somehow validate her words.

"Darling, that was Arthur Gilmore," Henry interjected gently, using the same fatherly tone he did with Miranda. "He rang earlier today about the same matter."

The color drained from Lois's face while she struggled to find a reply. A single tear broke free, tracing a silent path down her cheek before she gave up, turned sharply on her heel, and fled.

"Perhaps she isn't the right fit for the position," Cecil murmured, more to himself than anyone else. His gaze lingered on the empty spot where Lois had stood, his expression one of mild vexation.

"Give it time, Mr. Woolridge," Charles said, stepping forward with the warmth of the season wrapped around his words. Still in the Santa costume, he was every inch the embodiment of goodwill. "Everyone stumbles at first. Perhaps all she needs is a bit of guidance."

"Very well, very well," Cecil conceded with a nod. "After all, it wouldn't be in keeping with the holiday spirit to let the poor girl go just now. We shall see how the New Year turns her fortunes." He patted Charles on the shoulder in a gesture of appreciation.

"'Tis the season, after all." Cheeks still ruddy, Charles smoothed his beard. "I'll just slip out of this costume and head to the factory floor. We've much to prepare."

Henry sprung to attention. "I'll be right behind you once I've tidied up some odds and ends in my office," he said, a slight tightness at the corners of his mouth betraying a hint of urgency.

"Right so. Stella ought to be here any moment now," Cecil replied, glancing up at the ornate clock on the wall. "Frederick and I will accompany the family once she has arrived."

"And later," Charles added in a lower tone, "a discussion between the four of us is in order. I've come across something...rather interesting." He patted his pocket meaningfully before striding off.

Frederick approached the reception booth, peering behind a pile of overflowing boxes stacked behind it as though Lois might be hiding there. "I'll just call for a taxi myself, then," he declared.

"Frederick, my dear boy," Cecil chuckled, "a taxi may be your preference, but we have the numbers against us today."

"But Father, who wouldn't choose a peaceful ride over jostling around with the masses?" Frederick replied, a playful glint in his eye.

When Vera giggled as though at an inside joke, Rosemary raised a brow. "Everyone who goes back and forth between the factory and the offices has a different opinion about which route is preferable. Frederick, no surprise, values comfort over convenience."

"Comfort is a luxury for another day," Cecil replied with a note of gentle authority. "We'll take the elevated train, and that's settled."

"More's the pity," Frederick sighed with mock drama, though the edges of his lips twitched with amusement.

"Fortunately, I don't have to wait another day for luxury," Lady Foxworthy replied airily. "My driver is just outside. I imagine you'll manage without me squeezing into that crowded train." She breezed out, but almost as swiftly as the door closed behind her, it opened again.

"Stella!" Rosemary called out, spotting her younger sister. "You've finally made it, have you?"

"Just barely," Stella replied with a laugh, adjusting her coat as she joined the group and deposited a kiss on each of her parents' cheeks.

Except for the shape of her nose, which was pure Evelyn, Stella most resembled her father in coloring. Auburn hair, the same shade as her brother, Lionel's had been, framed doll-like features and porcelain skin while Rosemary and Frederick favored their mother. Miranda could more easily be mistaken for Rosemary's sister than Stella by someone who didn't know the family well.

"Shall we?" Cecil gestured towards the door, rallying the group with a decisive nod. "The train waits for no man—or woman."

As they made their way onto the street, Miranda suddenly stopped. "Oh, drat," she said, a note of embarrassment creeping into her voice. "I'm afraid I need to visit the loo before getting on the train. Why don't you go on ahead? I'll take the next one and meet you there."

"Go on, then," Cecil said, checking his pocket watch with a practiced air of patience. "But do try not to keep us waiting."

"Of course, Uncle," Miranda promised, turning with a swish of her skirt and swiftly departing.

Rosemary settled into her seat on the train as the car lurched forward. The city outside the window blurred into streaks of winter light, but only briefly before the motion sputtered to a halt with a sudden jolt.

"Apologies, ladies and gentlemen," the conductor's voice

crackled through the speaker. "A slight delay. We'll be on our way shortly."

"Shortly," Frederick snorted. "It's a good thing Miranda used the loo before she left. We could be here for days."

THREE

The sun cast long shadows across the courtyard when the Woolridge family finally arrived in front of the textile factory. Smoke in various shades of gray billowed out of the tall chimneys and into the crisp winter sky.

"We must look positively mental, marching down the street like a wedding procession," Rosemary remarked as they picked their way along the cobblestone pavement, Cecil and Frederick each flanked by two of the ladies, all four arms being utilized for stability.

"You're mental for wearing those shoes to a factory tour." Frederick's chortle cut off abruptly when he glanced at his wife and encountered her daggered gaze.

"I helped Rosemary choose those shoes," Vera said, quirking an elegant brow as if daring her husband to elaborate. Frederick declined.

Marriage hadn't tamed the couple's playful nature, Rosemary noted. And if there were any justice in the world, it never would. Her brother and oldest friend were a perfect match, even if it had taken them far too long to realize it.

Across the street from the south-facing side of the factory sat Lady Foxworthy in her swanky town car, comfortably swathed in luxurious furs that seemed to ward off more than just the day's chill.

"Ah, there you are," she called out with a playful lilt, peering over the rim of her spectacles. "I was beginning to think

I'd become the subject of a practical joke. It's been quite some time since I was stood up for a date, but it has been known to happen."

"Apologies, Beatrice," Cecil replied, offering a sheepish tip of his hat. "The train was uncharacteristically tardy this morning."

"Uncharacteristic, my right foot," Frederick interjected, his voice merry despite the complaint. "Precisely why I prefer the reliability of a good taxi."

Having heard this refrain more than once during their delayed train journey, Cecil offered a weary smile and chose not to engage. Instead, he surveyed his surroundings with a touch of unease.

"It seems no one else has arrived yet, so your timing remains impeccable," Lady Foxworthy reassured him.

Cecil's brow furrowed, a crease marring his usually composed face. "Odd, the tour was scheduled to begin by now," he murmured. "Where is everyone?"

Before they could speculate further, Miranda rounded the corner and approached at a clip, exuding confidence with every stride. Rosemary noticed she wore a sensible pair of flats but kept the observation to herself in lieu of offending Vera.

"Uncle Cecil, everyone," Miranda greeted with a nod. "I saw the commotion at the station and opted for a taxi instead. Evidently, the trains have been running late all morning. It seems schedules are more of a suggestion these days."

Frederick's grin widened, but his father didn't take the bait, instead smiling at Miranda with approval.

"Practical as always, dear."

The low purr of a well-tuned engine turned their attention as an almost identical sleek black motorcar rolled to a stop next to Lady Foxworthy's. Rosemary noted how her expression brightened at the sight of the vehicle and the way her eyes sparkled with unmistakable interest when a tall, solidly built gentleman about her age stepped out of the car. He tipped his hat in a gesture that would have been dashing if not contrasted by the lines of confusion etched on his face.

"Good day, Mr. Woolridge, Frederick," he called out. "I must admit, I've had quite the adventure this morning. I came here first, found no one about, then headed to the offices—only to be instructed to return here again."

"Apologies, Mr. Abernathy." Cecil offered a polite hand-shake and explained, "Our train ran late, yet it seems we're somehow still the first to arrive."

"Not to worry," Mr. Abernathy assured. "These things happen," he added vaguely, his attention diverted by the heat of Lady Foxworthy's gaze.

However, before introductions could be made, another figure appeared from around the corner, his stride brisk and purposeful. "Didn't see anyone out the front," he announced, running a hand through his unruly hair. "Tried my luck at the back, but the door was locked."

"Well, you didn't miss anything. It seems everyone is running behind the clock this morning," Frederick said, clapping the new arrival on the shoulder with friendly familiarity. "Everyone, this is Sam Drakeford."

Rosemary took in the man's slightly mismatched attire—his waistcoat clashed with his trousers, giving him a somewhat disheveled air. With a touch of amusement, she speculated that, like poor Uncle Henry, Mr. Drakeford must navigate the sartorial waters without the guidance of a wife's discerning eye. No woman would have let him out of the house wearing that tie.

Mr. Abernathy, on the other hand, looked neat as a pin in his stylishly cut suit, but his bare ring finger and general air of capability suggested he was the type of man who didn't need to be fussed over.

Frederick gestured towards the factory entrance. "Perhaps everyone else is inside. Shall we find out?"

Cecil nodded. "Let's."

Frederick led the group inside, where the air was much warmer and thick with the earthy perfume of oil and cotton. The factory floor sprawled in a grid of narrow aisles, flanked by rows of towering, iron-framed looms and spinning frames, their gears exposed and glistening with oil. Massive belts ran from floor to ceiling, winding through the machines like black snakes, while worn wooden floorboards shuddered beneath each relentless thud of machinery.

Henry emerged from one of the aisles, his expression of mild exasperation dissolving as his eyes landed on his brother and nephew. The rhythmic clacking of the looms nearly drowned out his voice as he called out, "There you are!"

"Couldn't be helped. I'm afraid our train was delayed," Cecil explained apologetically.

Henry shook his head, a wry smile playing at the corners of his mouth. "It seems punctuality has become a rare commodity these days. Is Charles with you, then?" His eyes roved over the group, brow furrowing when the search proved fruitless.

"We assumed he was here," Cecil replied, puzzled.

"Doesn't seem like Charles to be late, especially today," Frederick added, scratching his head. "He's put so much effort into planning this—into everything, really."

"How can he be late when he left before we did?"

"Might he have run into some trouble along the way?"

"Trouble?" Henry echoed, his voice edged with concern.

"Perhaps the same train woes that delayed us," Cecil suggested, though the uncertainty in his tone spoke volumes.

He glanced about, his expression a mix of confusion and concern before he decided with resolve, "I'm certain Charles would want us to carry on. Let's proceed with the tour."

Without missing a beat, Frederick slid into the role of guide and, eyes twinkling, addressed the assembled group. "It's been a whirlwind week, preparing for the holiday and tallying up inventory, so we thought it would be a good time for a tour—what with things being quieter than usual."

"Quieter?" Lady Foxworthy gestured at the still-bustling factory floor where machines chugged, and steam hissed like a mechanical chorus. "Your ears must already be on holiday, boy!"

"Ah, but it's usually much louder, Lady Beatrice. You see, we pause the engines every year to give our workers a break. It's a tradition woven into the fabric of this company as tightly as the threads in our textiles. Everyone here will be home with their families, receiving holiday pay from Christmas Eve through Boxing Day."

Cecil, his silver hair catching the soft glow of the factory lights, raised his voice to add, "It's the least we can do. None of this would be possible without their dedication. It doesn't matter how many machines you have if you don't have anyone to run them."

Rosemary noted an approving glance that passed between the two investors, making their respect for the family's commitment evident. It seemed the tour was already having the desired effect, and she felt a surge of optimism for the company's future.

The clatter of machinery was a dull roar in their ears as the investors scanned the busy floor where workers moved with practiced efficiency, narrated by Frederick's commentary.

"You're now standing in our packing and shipping area."

He gestured to the stacks of neatly wrapped bolts. "This is where the finished products come together, ready for distribution. We'll start here so you can see the end result of our work before we walk you through each stage of production. Next, we'll move to the carding section, where everything begins. Then it's on to spinning, where the raw fibers become threads, and finally, to the weaving floor, where you'll see our looms in action."

Frederick paused beside a ream of robust cloth unlike any Rosemary had seen used for clothing. "Here at Woolridge & Sons, we're not chasing the capricious whims of fashion."

"When do we meet the other son, old chap?"

When Frederick merely frowned, Mr. Abernathy clarified his question. "Woolridge & Sons."

Cecil cleared his throat. "We lost our Lionel to The Great War."

Embarrassed by the gaffe, Mr. Abernathy's face reddened slightly. "Apologies. I don't mean to pick at old wounds."

"That's quite all right," Cecil said, his tone gentle. "Between my brother's efforts and Frederick's keen eye for detail, we consider ourselves a family business in every sense of the word."

As if he hadn't been interrupted, Frederick continued his spiel. "Our focus is innovation and durability. We've expanded beyond run-of-the-mill fabric. These textiles"—he patted the sturdy material—"are designed to withstand the harshest of conditions, finding use in everything from industrial sails to military gear."

Rosemary watched as the investors leaned in, eyes alight with avid interest. Freddie's spiel made it clear that her family's business stood apart from the fading fortunes of other mills, embracing change rather than shunning it.

"Remarkable," Sam Drakeford murmured, brushing his fingers against the coarse weave. "And quite the departure from my own line of luxury weaves. Diversification seems not only prudent but, indeed, exciting."

"Quite so," echoed Mr. Abernathy, though with a hint of something else in his tone—a recognition of opportunity, perhaps. His gaze lingered on the bolts of material. "These creations might never grace the pages of British Vogue, but they hold the promise of weathering both storms and time—an allure of a different, more enduring type."

"A lovely compliment," Frederick replied, pleased.

Lady Foxworthy was the only one in the group who appeared unmoved. She fanned her face with a gloved hand. "Perhaps it's quieter than usual, but is it always this warm?"

Before Frederick could reply, her eyes rolled skyward as she fainted, spilling into the arms of a shocked Mr. Abernathy.

FOUR

Mr. Abernathy's strong arms caught the poor woman before she could hit the floor, cradling her against his chest. "Lady Foxworthy!" he exclaimed, his composure nearly shaken. "Are you ill?"

Slowly, her eyelids fluttered open, and she blinked up at him, momentarily disoriented.

"I... I'm quite all right," she said finally, her voice wavering slightly as she regained her bearings.

"Are you certain?" he asked, keeping a steadying hand on her elbow when she made to stand. "Perhaps it would be best if I escort you to your car."

"No, no, that won't be necessary. Despite appearances, I am no wilting flower, Mr. Abernathy." Lady Foxworthy drew herself up to her full height, a determined glint returning to her eye.

Rosemary watched the exchange with avid interest, unsurprised to see a similar reaction from most of the rest of the group. "This is better than dinner theater," Vera whispered.

"Well, then," Frederick began once Lady Foxworthy had been set to rights. "It seems we ought to have discussed safety first and foremost." He gestured towards the behemoths of iron and steel that surrounded them. "Heat is a constant companion here, along with dehydration and fatigue. We take great care to look after our workers, ensuring ample hydration breaks and monitoring for signs of exhaustion."

"We also handle a medley of chemicals for dyeing and bleaching—necessary for quality but dangerous if mishandled. Not to mention the gears and belts; they've been known to snag more than just thread. Keep your hands to yourselves if you don't want to lose them."

Rosemary noticed how Frederick's lively eyes sobered at the mention of potential danger. His concern raised hers as she envisioned hapless workers caught in the relentless dance of cog and spindle.

Dreading the answer, she asked, "Have there been many accidents?"

"The odd slip with shears or a weaving hook. We use what's called a Flying Shuttle." Moving quickly, Frederick retrieved an object from a nearby basket. Boat-shaped with a conical steel point on either end, the wooden device cradled a bobbin that trailed yarn.

He tossed the shuttle to Rosemary, who hefted it in her hand as if weighing it. "And this is dangerous?" She couldn't see how.

"It can be. A motor driven apparatus pushes the shuttles back and forth through the warp channels at great speed. With that much force, the pointed end would pierce the skin with a bullet-like force should one escape the machine."

Rosemary handed the shuttle back to him, fascinated by the things she'd learned about her family's business.

As Frederick continued his tour, expertly delineating the stages of production, Rosemary felt a swell of pride for her brother's confidence. He might wear it as a veneer over the somewhat feckless hedonist she knew still lurked underneath, but that didn't matter a whit. People could be more than one thing—it was a lesson she had only recently learned about herself yet knew without a doubt applied to others as well.

Drakeford's eyes gleamed with the cunning honed from years within the folds of family business. "Your American venture holds great promise," he remarked. "A coup, if I may say so. One that will push at least one major competitor out of the market."

"Innovation always does," Mr. Abernathy said, nodding sagely. "Especially when paired with shrewd business decisions, as seems to be the practice here at Woolridge & Sons. Furthermore, I admire your commitment to your charitable endeavors. Philanthropy is a privilege afforded by prudence."

His praise drew a sigh from Lady Foxworthy, whose hand still rested in the crook of his arm despite the color having fully returned to her face.

"You're too kind, Mr. Abernathy," she gushed, accepting the compliment as if it had been meant for her. "Practically a saint."

"Hardly," Mr. Abernathy replied with a hint of amusement. "I enjoy the finer things in life as much as anyone else, and luxury is another privilege I'm happy to indulge."

Amid the interplay of subtle flattery and coy glances, Rosemary caught sight of her uncle hovering at the fringes of the conversation. Poor Henry, constantly yearning yet ever silent, stood awkwardly with hands clasped behind his back—a silent suitor watching helplessly as Lady Foxworthy's interest deepened with each syllable Abernathy uttered.

Her eyelashes fluttered as she gazed up at him. "You can't take it with you, can you?"

"Quite right," Mr. Abernathy agreed with a hint of roguish charm. "That's why I eat at the most highly-rated restaurants and stay in the best hotels. For instance, the one I booked for my stay in London puts on an elaborate Christmas do. They charge exorbitant rates, of course, but life is short, after all."

Lady Foxworthy's gaze lingered on him for a long moment before she replied, "And happiness is hard to come by. We must seize our opportunities when we find them."

"Seize indeed, Lady Foxworthy," Rosemary muttered the comment quietly enough for only Vera to hear.

The hum of the machinery dulled somewhat as Frederick stopped before a closed door labeled *Research & Development*. "Now, ladies and gentlemen, we come to the cornerstone of Woolridge & Sons' success—the Research and Development department. This is where the real magic happens, where the ideas are born, nurtured, and brought to life."

With a flourish, he pushed open the door, revealing a space that buzzed with an energy quite different from the rhythmic thrum of the factory floor. In one corner sat a woman whose presence was as crisp and professional as the neatly stacked papers on her desk.

"Ah, and this is Eleanor, invaluable coordinator for all our R&D conundrums," Frederick announced with a flourish.

"Keeping the men in line, no doubt," Sam Drakeford quipped, his tone suggesting a double meaning behind the words.

"Quite, Sir," Eleanor replied in a voice that similarly managed to be both polite and razor-sharp. Her gaze connected briefly with Rosemary's, her eyes filled with a steely resolve that made it clear her role encompassed far more than its title suggested. Looking around curiously, she asked, "Where is Mr. Harrington?"

"We're not entirely certain," Cecil replied. "We haven't seen him and thought perhaps he'd encountered an emergency. I take it you haven't heard from him either?"

Eleanor's brow furrowed with concern. "Not since this morning before he left for the office. I expected him to return before the tour commenced, but he never arrived. He's been preparing for this for weeks. I can't imagine what could have kept him." It was a phrase that had been uttered too many times already.

"Let us not dwell on Charles's absence," Frederick interjected, attempting to steer the conversation back to a more positive note. "Eleanor, perhaps you could tell us a little about what goes on here in his stead?"

"Of course." Surprised, Eleanor nodded and, with a glint of pride in her eye, launched into an explanation. "Here in R&D, it's our job to dream up innovations in textile production while striving to improve efficiency, quality, and design. We bring together art and science, form and function, to engineer the fabrics of the future. It's a creative process, but one that's not always tidy or linear."

She gestured to the table in the center of the room, its surface obscured by a riot of sketches, formulas, and samples in every imaginable hue. "At first glance, this may look like a jumble of disparate elements, but in reality, it's a carefully curated collection of our most promising ideas. Each swatch, each sketch represents hours of experimentation and refinement."

"We start with the fibers themselves, always looking for ways to improve upon nature's design. Take this sample, for instance," she said, picking up a swatch of fabric that shimmered with an iridescent sheen. "It's a new blend of silk and a synthetic fiber we've developed. Stronger than steel by weight, yet as soft and supple as a rose petal."

She passed it around and moved on to another sample, this one a rich, deep blue. "And this? Dyed using a new process that not only produces more vibrant, longer-lasting color, but does so using a fraction of the water and chemicals of traditional methods. And that's just the start of what Woolridge & Sons have to offer."

Amid a chorus of oohs and ahhs as the guests ran their fingers over the various swatches, Eleanor stepped back from the group as if trying to fade into the wallpaper.

"Thank you, Eleanor. You're truly one of our most valuable resources, and we appreciate your insight," Frederick said warmly before returning his attention to the tour. "Now, let's press on," he implored. "We still have much to show you, including an area of the factory currently being renovated. I'm sure you'll find it quite interesting."

He ushered the group out of the R&D department and towards the rear of the building. As they meandered through the maze of narrow aisles, Mr. Abernathy remarked, "Frederick, your presentation has been extraordinary. If I'm being honest, I can't envision anyone but you taking charge of the American venture. You have the makings of a fine executive." His eyes shined with enthusiasm.

"Thank you for your kind words," Frederick replied modestly, "but rest assured, Charles Harrington has been instrumental here. He has the vision to drive innovation forward—a true asset. And, he's half American, which makes him perfectly suited to take charge across the pond," Frederick continued, seamlessly redirecting attention from the awkward exchange.

Ignoring Frederick's response, Sam Drakeford said, "You do seem to be the man for it. I've never had much faith in Americans—no offense intended—but we'd do well to keep British minds at the helm. It's our enterprise, after all."

Rosemary caught the briefest hint of distaste on her brother's face before he masked it with a congenial smile. "While I fancy a baseball match l as much as the next chap, I had quite enough of New York during our last holiday."

"There's no such thing as too much New York," Miranda stated emphatically, receiving an approving nod from Mr. Abernathy.

Frederick shrugged. "Regardless, the wife and I just settled into our new home here..."

"And, of course, you must be planning on starting a family soon, no?" Lady Foxworthy interjected with a knowing glance towards Vera just as the group approached a particularly intricate assembly line.

"Oh, well, you know how it is," Frederick sputtered, attempting to keep his tone light. "We're in no hurry, but we are finding ourselves rather fond of the fresh coat of paint and the way the morning light spills into the—"

His sentence hung unfinished, the last word evaporating as he led the group around the next corner. The expression on his face halted any further inquiry from Lady Foxworthy regarding domestic bliss.

A collective gasp cut through the sudden stillness. Rosemary's heart skipped a beat, then began to race as she rose gingerly on tiptoes to look over her brother's shoulder. The acrid scent of iron riding heavy on the air made her nostrils twitch before her eyes landed on the grim tableau.

There he was—Charles Harrington, or what was left of him —sprawled unceremoniously on the cold factory floor.

Frederick found his voice. "It seems you were right, Mr. Abernathy. Life is quite short, indeed."

FIVE

Rosemary stared down at Charles' lifeless body. His eyes were glassy and vacant, fixed on some far-off point beyond the ceiling. She shuddered, swallowing down the knot that lodged in her throat as the mingled scents of blood and machinery oil filled her nostrils.

"Good heavens!" Evelyn's hand flew up to cover her mouth as soon as the exclamation escaped her lips.

"Bloody hell." Sam Drakeford repeated the sentiment, his face going from ashen white to a sickly shade of green—not that anyone could fault him. The crimson pool surrounding Charles's limp form crept slowly outward, but Rosemary noted that the blood had sprayed primarily towards the wall, leaving behind a ghastly mural.

Shivering, she looked around for any indication that the deep wound in the side of his head might have been the result of a tragic accident, but it was obvious that all of the machines in the vicinity had been dormant for quite some time, mute witnesses to the tragedy unfolding among them.

It took a great effort for Rosemary to force away the whispers of danger and intrigue already playing at the edges of her consciousness and focus instead on cataloging all the details of the scene that might prove crucial when it came time to sift through alibis and accusations. Around the body, the floor was littered with bolts of fabric and half-finished weaves, strewn about as if by someone in a panic or a rage.

Miranda stood like a marble statue amid the chaos, hands folded neatly in front of her, much like a soprano preparing to hit a high note at the opera. If Rosemary had been inclined to bed, she might have put down a few shillings on the fact that her cousin was poised to let loose a scream.

Henry's jaw clenched so tightly the muscle in his cheek twitched, his eyes glued to Charles Harrington's crumpled form. Rosemary noted a tremor in his hand—a rarity for a man known for his unflappable nature. Seeing his daughter's distress, he subtly tapped his cheek in a gesture quite familiar to members of the Woolridge family.

Meeting her father's gaze, Miranda straightened her spine as if bolstered by his silent command to "Chin up." In the split second before her expression smoothed over, she looked at Rosemary, her eyes showing deep wells of sorrow.

"Rather an unfortunate development. Poor Charles." Mr. Abernathy's stoicism found a counterpart in Lady Foxworthy, whose wide eyes betrayed a morbid curiosity she couldn't quite conceal. Moreover, she appeared invigorated by the circumstances despite having recently fainted.

The eerie silence fractured with a wail when Eleanor from R&D stumbled into view. Her face crumpled like tissue paper as she collapsed to her knees, the sounds of her sobs echoing off stone and steel. Raw and guttural, in contrast to the Woolridges' composed grief, the sound tore at Rosemary's heart.

"Charles... Oh, God, not Charles..." As Eleanor's voice broke, thick with anguish, Miranda appraised her with an expression caught between bewilderment and disapproval. Evelyn's response needed no such distinction. Any outward show of emotion was deemed unacceptable, though Rosemary noted her mother appeared a bit green around the gills herself.

Cecil slipped a protective arm around his wife while Vera did the same for Eleanor, as if a mere embrace could shield either woman from the brutal reality before her. "Vera, perhaps you could escort her back to R&D," Cecil suggested gently.

"Stella, dear, go with them," Evelyn added. For once, Stella had the sense not to argue with her mother and instead moved swiftly to help Vera guide Eleanor away from the scene. Surprisingly, Miranda followed, almost as if in a trance.

Once the sobs subsided into silence, Cecil addressed the remainder of the group.

"Please accept my deepest apologies for this...unfortunate turn of events." His voice was steady yet tinged with sorrow. Everyone clustered together, their earlier excitement replaced with hushed murmurs and furtive glances. "Shall we table our business for the moment?"

"Now there, Woolridge, you can't be blamed for such barbarism," Thomas Abernathy declared, his voice cutting through the whispered speculation. "I've seen my share of dark days and know we must rise above them. Despite such tragedy, this deal holds promise, and I intend to stay the course until the holidays—and whatever ghastly business this is—are concluded."

Sam Drakeford, who had been shifting uneasily, stepped forward. His face was pale, his eyes darting like a cornered animal's. "Promises be damned," he blurted, his voice quivering. "If this is the sort of calamity that shadows Woolridge & Sons, I must reconsider my investment."

His words hung in the air, more chilling than the draft that seeped through the factory's windows. Rosemary couldn't help but notice how Drakeford avoided looking directly at Charles' body as if the sight would burn his retinas.

"Come now," Frederick interjected, attempting a diplomatic calm, "let's not make hasty decisions in the wake of tragedy. Clarity will return when the authorities have sorted out this dreadful affair."

Lady Foxworthy leaned towards Evelyn, her voice dropping to a whisper intended for gossip yet loud enough for Rosemary to overhear.

"Steadfast as a ship in a storm," Lady Foxworthy's gaze lingered on Mr. Abernathy, her features softening. "Some men possess a certain fortitude, even in chaos."

Evelyn's nod was measured, and Rosemary detected a layer of subtext in her mother's reply. "Indeed, Beatrice," Evelyn said softly.

Their conversation was cut short by the heavy clunk of the factory doors swinging open, letting in a gust of winter air along with Max's familiar visage. Only now, he was the solid presence of Chief Inspector Whittington, surveying the scene with an air of authority, keen eyes taking in every detail until they found what they were searching for.

When they landed on Rosemary, he strode her way, brow furrowed with concern. He removed his hat as he approached and offered a reassuring smile. "We really must stop meeting like this."

"Max." Rosemary greeted him with a weak smile of her own. "I didn't expect you to arrive so quickly."

"Murder has a way of drawing swift attention," he noted dryly. He leaned slightly closer and lowered his voice. "Let's wrap this one up quickly, shall we? I had hoped to spend the holidays under the mistletoe, not looming over corpses."

"Infinitely more romantic," Rosemary agreed, appreciating his ability to inject a moment of levity into even the darkest situations.

Sam Drakeford's eyes widened in astonishment, the gears in his mind visibly grinding to a halt as he processed Rosemary's familiarity with Max. "You know the chief inspector?" he blurted out, incredulity lacing his tone. "And not just in passing, but...?"

When the question hung in the air for a long moment, Cecil answered for her. "My daughter has solved several murder cases." The pride in his voice brought a blush to Rosemary's cheeks.

"Must be terribly unpleasant to find yourself amidst such grisly scenes repeatedly," Drakeford muttered, taking a step back, his face pale as if he'd seen a ghost—or rather, the unfortunate result of one's earthly departure. "What a dreadful habit."

"I've often wondered if it's a habit or a curse," Rosemary replied wryly. Sam paled even further, seemingly disturbed by the thought, and then, with a final, queasy look at Charles Harrington's lifeless form, clutched his handkerchief and excused himself, retreating around the corner where the sounds of his discomfort echoed faintly.

Rosemary grimaced, grateful he'd sicked up there and not on her shoes.

She turned her attention to Max, who knelt beside the corpse, his trained eyes scanning for any clue that might point to the perpetrator.

"We found him like this," Rosemary explained, her voice steady despite the gruesome sight. "No one touched the body, but I noticed the direction of the blood spray. It indicates the assailant likely got away fairly clean."

Max nodded in approval. "That's a very astute observation, Rosemary. The angle of the spray does suggest the killer managed to avoid the worst of it." He crouched down, pulling a small magnifying glass from his coat pocket to examine the floor around Charles' body in minute detail.

His gaze swept methodically over the dusty concrete, taking in every scuff and smudge.

"What's this?" Max leaned in closer, his nose nearly touching the floor. "Rosemary, take a look."

She knelt beside him, following his gaze to a faint but unmistakable streak of blood, barely visible against the grime-coated concrete. At the end closest to Charles's body, the edges of a partial shoe print stood out in sharp relief.

"Maybe our killer didn't get away so clean after all," Max mused, carefully positioning his magnifying glass over the print. "It's not much, but it's a start." He stood up, a determined glint in his eye. "It's time we had a look at some shoe soles."

A murmur rippled through the group as each person reluctantly complied, lifting their feet for inspection. Rosemary watched, noting their various responses as, one by one, they revealed their soles—leather, polished and scuffed—none bearing the damning stain.

"Curious," Max muttered, his gaze lingering momentarily on Sam Drakeford, who had just returned, looking paler than before. But even his expensive brogues were pristine.

Rosemary nodded, her eyes flicking to Lady Foxworthy, who still clung to Mr. Abernathy's arm, her expression serene despite the gruesome scene. "Did you notice anyone unusual, Beatrice?" she asked, keeping her tone light despite the tension in the air. "While you were waiting on the street this morning?"

"Darling, I hardly paid attention," Lady Foxworthy confessed, fluttering her lashes theatrically. "I was quite absorbed in my latest novella. But now that you mention it, no one particularly suspicious caught my eye."

"Sir," the young constable's voice cut through the conversation. "The medical examiner has arrived and will be in shortly."

Max nodded crisply. "Why don't we clear a path for him? Hawkins, I need you to take statements from everyone in the factory this morning. Start with the tour guests and then interview the factory staff. We need to establish a timeline and determine who had access to this area. I'll speak with Mrs. Lillywhite myself."

He turned to the guests, letting his gaze fall on each in turn, "You'll each give your statements to Constable Hawkins, but if anyone knows anything useful about Charles Harrington and why someone might want him dead, speak now."

Cecil stepped forward, his brow furrowed with concern. "Charles was well-liked by everyone who knew him," he said, his voice tinged with disbelief. "He was a kind, generous man who always went out of his way to help others. It seems incomprehensible that someone would want him dead."

He turned to Henry, seeking confirmation in his brother's eyes. Henry met his gaze, his expression somber as he swallowed hard. "To my knowledge, no one had a problem with Charles," he corroborated, his voice low but firm. "He was respected by the workers and admired by his peers. This...this doesn't make any sense."

Even Sam Drakeford nodded, though his expression was tinged with reluctance. "I've made no bones about my feelings regarding Americans, but in my limited dealings with Harrington, he was always proper. Perhaps a bit rigid, but a sound choice for the role." It wasn't the impression Rosemary had, given Drakeford's earlier comment regarding Americans, and she filed the fact away for later contemplation.

"Same goes for me," Mr. Abernathy agreed. "Charles

seemed a thoroughly upstanding fellow. A damn shame, to be certain."

Even Frederick's usual lighthearted demeanor was shaken. "His loss leaves a hole that won't be easily filled."

With nothing more to say, the rest of the group filed out.

Rosemary hung back, her gaze lingering on what was left of the man poised to lead Woolridge & Sons into a promising new era. Now, the American expansion teetered on the edge of ruin, overshadowed by this violent act. And with so much at stake—the family's reputation, the future of the business—all of it hung by a thread more delicate than the finest spun wool.

"Tell me everything you know." Max's voice cut through her reverie.

"Right then," Rosemary began confidently, having already rehearsed it in her head several times. "Charles left the offices in Bloomsbury at half past one this afternoon, and the tour began just after three o'clock. The window of opportunity is narrow. It must have been when we were all delayed on that wretched train—Father and Frederick included—" She met Max's gaze, a measure of relief evident in her eyes, "leaving only a handful of people here unsupervised."

Max nodded, making quick notes in his small black book. "Alibis?"

"None that we had time to discover," Rosemary admitted, tucking a loose lock of flaxen hair behind her ear as she considered. "Same goes for opportunity. Everyone present for the tour was either busy with preparations or delayed by the trains."

"We can't rule out anyone yet—not until we have a fuller picture. The factory staff?"

"Reduced for the occasion," she replied, lowering her voice to a conspiratorial murmur. "Fewer workers mean fewer suspects—or at least, it would seem that way. This section of the factory is under renovation."

Max scanned the room, calculating, and continued firing off questions. "And the victim? Any known enemies or grudges?"

"You heard what everyone said. By all accounts, he was a model employee," Rosemary answered thoughtfully. "Promotion on the horizon, well-liked by his peers. Perhaps he was too perfect—envy always lurks in the shadows of success."

"Jealousy can be a powerful motive." Max tapped his pen against his chin thoughtfully.

"Max," Rosemary said, her voice low and urgent, "this doesn't seem like premeditated malice. It's too...messy."

"Agreed," he replied. "I think the killer acted on the spur of the moment—a crime of passion or rage."

"Either way, they likely had close ties to Charles." Rosemary hoped the motive wasn't woven as tightly as the company's innovative weaves. "One doesn't resort to this type of violence over an acquaintance."

Rosemary and Max rejoined the group just as Miranda finished giving her statement to the constable. Her face was composed, but Rosemary noticed a slight tremble in her hands as she smoothed her skirt. Henry placed a comforting hand on his daughter's shoulder.

"I'll take you home, darling," he said gently. "You've been through quite an ordeal."

But Miranda shook her head, a determined set to her jaw. "No, Father, I'm quite all right. I think I'd like a moment to myself if you don't mind."

Henry looked as though he might protest, but a sharp glance from his daughter silenced him. With a nod, he stepped back, allowing her to pass, but he watched her walk away through the empty factory with sorrow in his eyes.

Max turned to the remaining Woolridges. "It's been a trying day. I'll be by later this evening to question the family further, but for now, I think it's best if you all go home and try to get some rest. We'll continue our investigation here and speak with the rest of the staff tomorrow."

Six

With unwavering duty, the hands of the ornate grandfather clock in the corner of Rosemary's parlor ticked away the seconds for what felt like an eternity while she and the rest of the family awaited Max's arrival. Her artist's eye saw them as a portrait of nervous anticipation, draped across settees and chairs with a restlessness that belied the comforting crackle of the fireplace. Perched upright on the edge of a tufted ottoman, Stella twirled a lock of auburn hair around her finger until she noticed her mother's disapproving gaze and abruptly stilled.

"We ought to be being seated at Kettner's right now," Evelyn commented when six o'clock rolled around with still no word, and the clock rang out the hour in time to the rumbling of stomachs. "How much longer do you suppose the inspector will be?" she asked testily.

Rosemary shrugged, annoyed even though the same question had been playing through her thoughts on a loop for over an hour. "Max is good at his job, or else he wouldn't have been made Chief Inspector. You need to trust him."

"Of course, I trust Max, Rosemary," her mother sputtered, "His integrity has never been in question."

"I'm sure he's simply taking his time and gathering all the evidence he can before returning with news."

Evelyn's jaw clenched, but before she could formulate a further retort, Cecil piped up to inquire hopefully, "I don't suppose your cook left behind any more of those mince pies, did she?"

Frederick visibly perked at the notion.

"I'll go check." Grateful for the chance to escape, Rosemary excused herself, Vera and Stella following behind.

Vera donned an apron in the kitchen while Rosemary stared at her in surprise.

"What?" Vera said, tilting her head in challenge. "You don't think I know how to warm a pie? I've been cooking for Frederick, and he's not gone to skin and bones yet."

It took an effort to drag her chin back up from where it had landed when her mouth dropped open, but Rosemary managed the task with no small amount of aplomb. "You know very well that I have every faith in you, Vera. It's just that I've never seen you in an apron before."

Flipping her dark hair back with a shake of her head, Vera cocked a hip and struck a pose. "I think I pull off the look quite nicely. Freddie seems to like it well enough."

"I'm certain he does." And that was all Rosemary had to say on the subject. Instead of digging the conversational hole deeper, she opened the icebox to retrieve Gladys's leftover mince pies and arranged them on the baking tray Stella had found in one of the cupboards.

After checking the temperature to ensure it wasn't too hot, Vera slid the tray into the piping oven like she'd done it a hundred times before. "Ten minutes ought to do it," she said. "We don't want to bake them again, only to warm them enough to eat."

The way she wiped her hands on her apron finally struck a chord with Rosemary. With a snap of her fingers, she exclaimed, "I see! You're learning to cook because you're auditioning for another play."

Eyes alight with humor, Vera shook her head. "I'm not auditioning for anything," she declared but quickly relented. "Because I didn't have to. The producer offered me the part, and yes, it is the starring role."

"Congratulations," Stella said. "You're a shoo-in."

"Practically perfect in every way," Rosemary agreed with an affectionate smile. "Now, tell us all about it."

Filled with details about Vera's upcoming play, the allotted ten minutes had nearly passed when Rosemary said, "I do hope Max arrives soon. Had I known we'd be this long without news, I might have convinced him to let me stay."

Stella's lips firmed. Until that moment, Rosemary had never noticed a strong resemblance between her sister and her mother, but their disapproving looks, she now realized, were precisely the same. "Did you not only a few minutes ago tell Mother not to borrow trouble? Let Max do his job, and try to put it out of your mind."

"Easier said than done," Rosemary said, not bothering to argue the rest of her point. Stella wouldn't understand what it felt like to see all of the pieces of evidence spread out like a puzzle or the flash of intuition that came at the moment of solving a crime.

"You'll feel better once you've eaten."

Vera's promise proved true for everyone. Her appetite dulled by the delicious pie, Rosemary had nearly stopped fretting when a sharp rap at the door finally announced Max's arrival.

"Evening all." His voice carried the weight of London's fog-laden air as he stepped over the threshold, a leather holdall full of files clutched in his hand. His eyes, when they met Rosemary's, carried a silent message of trust. "I've brought updates on the progress of Charles's murder investigation."

"It seems there is a first time for everything," she jested lightly, a wry lilt in her voice that softened the gravity of the situation.

Max's lips curled into what, under other circumstances, would have been an amused smirk as he surveyed the familial scene. "We both know your involvement is inevitable, so I'll be as transparent as possible."

Evelyn offered him a surprisingly warm nod devoid of her usual frostiness. "Max, I must say, your dedication to this dreadful business is commendable." Rosemary wondered briefly if the comment had been made for her benefit as much as his, but her mother continued to avoid her gaze.

"Thank you, Mrs. Woolridge," Max replied, raising a cautious brow at her change in demeanor. "But I'm afraid some of my news won't be well-received." He hesitated, glancing towards Cecil before continuing. "As you've probably already guessed, the factory can't reopen until we finish our preliminary investigation."

Cecil nodded. "That's as I expected."

"Additionally," Max said, his tone firm despite the note of apology weaving through it, "I'll need you all to stay in London. Given the circumstances, it would be wise to prepare to remain in the city at least through Boxing Day."

The weight of altered holiday plans settled over the family like December frost on the windowpanes, but Stella appeared quite chuffed and clapped her hands with glee. "Then it's settled! I'll ring Leonard and have him bring the children here for Christmas!"

"You'd better do it quickly," Max warned. "There's a storm brewing that might make traveling in and out of the city rather difficult."

"Very well," Evelyn interjected with a note of practicality, her pearls glinting under the chandelier's light. "I suppose we could arrange to stay at that hotel Mr. Abernathy spoke so highly of."

Sitting beside Frederick, Vera exchanged a quick, wounded look with Rosemary; the suggestion clearly stung. But before their mother could elaborate, Frederick stepped in, his tone gallant and tinged with pride. "Nonsense! Our home has just been done up for the season—fresh garlands, fires in every hearth. It'll be cozy enough to warm any chilled spirit. You shall all stay with us."

"Frederick, that's a splendid idea," Rosemary said brightly. "I dare say it'll be a holiday none of us will soon forget."

"Just think, Evelyn!" Vera exclaimed. "Christmas in London. We'll have a tree, presents, dinner—it will be positively Dickensian!" She sighed, her eyes turning misty at the scene playing out in her imagination.

"But who will do the cooking and the cleaning up?" Evelyn demanded. "At the moment, neither of you have any help to speak of."

Ice tinkled against glass as Frederick swirled his drink and raised one eyebrow. "Do I not recall you insisting you could get along quite well without a troupe of maids?"

"Surely I didn't mean at Christmas—" Evelyn began to protest, but Frederick cut her off.

"Surely four capable ladies such as yourselves can figure out how to prepare a few meals for the family. The shop down the street ought to have everything you require, and they'll even deliver it—quite quickly if you tip well," he added when she still appeared doubtful.

For a long moment, the pair were caught in a mother-son standoff.

"Mother, it'll be an adventure!" Stella's voice carried an

edge of encouragement that earned her nothing more than a disapproving, purse-lipped glare.

Even Evelyn Woolridge recognized when she'd been defeated. "Given the circumstances," she finally sighed, "I suppose we can manage without the staff. After all, what is life without the occasional challenge to overcome?"

"I'll notify the press," Frederick said cheekily. "I'm sure they'll want to send their best reporter to cover your inspiring tale of triumph over adversity."

Surprisingly, Cecil managed to keep from smiling at the comment. "Then it's settled," he said diplomatically, laying the matter to rest. "Let us return to the matter at hand."

Max, ever the meticulous inspector, cleared his throat. "Regarding Mr. Harrington's unfortunate demise," he began, capturing the attentive silence of the Woolridge family, "one factory worker reported seeing him arrive and head towards the research and development area shortly before his death."

The factory's layout unfolded in Rosemary's mind as she retraced what had probably been Charles's last steps.

"Henry arrived not long after but went in the opposite direction," Max continued. "His statement claims he made a sweep of the factory grounds as a precaution before the scheduled tour. The good news is several workers corroborate his account. He was seen making the rounds, checking the premises."

Something about Max's tone raised the hair on the back of Rosemary's neck. "Is there bad news, then? Is Uncle Henry a legitimate suspect?" Her voice sounded thinner than toilet tissue.

"Everyone is a legitimate suspect in the eyes of the law," Max hedged, his brow creasing into a line he feared was becoming a permanent wrinkle. Or maybe a target, given the daggered look Rosemary aimed at him. "Unfortunately, their statements don't entirely eliminate the possibility that he could have murdered Charles during that time."

"Good old Uncle Henry doesn't have the gumption for blunt force," Frederick said, exchanging a troubled glance with his father.

Rosemary pictured her Uncle Henry, a man more comfortable with accounts than altercations, and weighed the thought of him harboring murderous intent. As Frederick had said, the image simply didn't fit.

Cecil, his face etched with concern, finally spoke. "It wouldn't be proper for me to speculate. But truly, my brother is more likely to wilt under pressure than exert it. It's difficult to picture him having the mettle to bludgeon poor Charles to death."

"For what reason? Nothing about Charles' death benefits Uncle Henry. If anything, it heaps a pile of work on his shoulders. You can't think he had anything to do with murder." Rosemary watched Max closely while he formulated his response. She'd come to know him well enough by now to pick up on the subtle clues that revealed his thoughts.

"Regardless of what I find likely, everyone present will need to be questioned—your Uncle Henry, the investors, the employees. Take comfort knowing it's too early to settle on any one person."

Rosemary's heart clenched at the thought of her mild-mannered uncle being prodded with questions, but she knew Max was right. Sentiment had no place in a murder investigation. Besides, Max wasn't the type to browbeat a false confession out of someone ill-equipped to handle the pressure.

"You're barking up the wrong tree with Uncle Henry, old chap," Frederick paced before the hearth, his fingers drumming against his lips in contemplation. The room's warmth did little to quell the chill of uncertainty that had settled over them like an unwelcome fog. "But I suppose you have to start somewhere."

"If I had to choose between them, I'd expect cousin Miranda to be the one with the stomach for violence," Rosemary mused aloud, earning herself a patented Evelyn Woolridge glare.

"Who said you needed to choose?" Evelyn demanded. "Must any of the family members need to be postulated as a murderer?"

"Haven't you been listening, Mother? The police will have to, so we might as well do the same," Rosemary said, pressing on. "Don't forget, Miranda wasn't nestled among us on that train carriage during the time of the murder. She had opportunity aplenty and knows the factory's corridors better than most."

"Opportunity, perhaps," Frederick conceded, "but what of motive? Miranda has shown little interest in the gears of business, only in the golden fruits it yields."

After a quick moment of thought, Rosemary snapped her fingers. "She loves America. She always talked about visiting when we were children, and don't you remember Freddie—she said there was no such thing as too much New York."

Evelyn remained unconvinced. "Why on earth would that suggest she murdered Mr. Harrington?"

Exasperated, Rosemary explained, "If Uncle Henry was named head of the American division, she could have accompanied him. It would have been a dream come true—not just a visit, but a chance to live in the States. Miranda is used to getting what she wants, after all, and doesn't tend to take it well when she doesn't."

Frederick opened his mouth as if to protest further but closed it again.

Max shook his head. "You're forgetting how much strength it takes to bludgeon a grown man to death. It's doubtful a woman would have had the fortitude. I'd hazard our guilty party is a man."

Stella shook her golden curls even more decidedly. "I wouldn't be so sure, Inspector. Why, I've read stories of adrenaline-fueled mothers lifting automobiles clear off the ground to save their trapped children. In the heat of a passionate moment, a woman could certainly find the strength to commit a violent act, especially if she felt threatened or betrayed."

"She has a point," Rosemary agreed, her eyes glinting with a sudden intensity.

"Well, then," Vera interjected, "let us also not overlook matters of the heart. Charles was an eligible bachelor, affable and esteemed. Could there have been a dalliance, a spurned affection?" Coming from her, the theory sounded like the plot of a drama fit to be played out on stage.

"I appreciate your desire to be thorough," Max said in the voice Rosemary had heard him use to calm more than one jittery suspect. "However, Charles appears to have been a fairly private person. So far, nobody seems to know anything about his personal life, but rest assured, we're looking into it."

He turned his attention to Cecil and Frederick. "Did anyone have a grudge against him? Had he angered or offended anyone? Perhaps one of the factory workers or the chaps from his department?"

Frederick glanced at his father. "None of the factory workers would have been threatened by Charles's success, and he treated everyone fairly. I can't imagine what other cause they'd have to want him dead."

Max's eyes narrowed thoughtfully as he considered the information. "What about Woolridge & Sons itself? Any rivals or competitors who might hold a grudge?"

"None that we know of," Cecil replied slowly, "but Charles was the keystone of our expansion plans. He could navigate both worlds—American and British—with ease. It made him invaluable, which, in light of the situation, might have also made him a target."

"What about the investors?" Rosemary asked. "Thomas Abernathy and Sam Drakeford are the only other people who were close enough to be on the spot at the time of the murder. We were on the train, after all. We don't know what happened during that time, and Lady Foxworthy admitted she wasn't paying attention to who went in or out of the factory. Mr. Abernathy took the dead body in stride—unlike Sam Drakeford, who doesn't appear to have the stomach for murder."

Frederick leaned against the mantelpiece. "Rest assured, Rosie, we've been through the investors with a fine-toothed comb. I'm not denying Abernathy's as slick as they come, but his ledger books? Spotless. His accountants strike just the right chord of efficiency without desperation. It's the precise balance Henry admires."

"Efficiency without desperation," Rosemary repeated softly, mulling over the phrase. She could almost see the numbers lining up in obedient rows, concealing nothing—or perhaps everything—behind their sterile precision. "And Drakeford?"

"Grew up steeped in the textile trade," Cecil answered. "His father was a decent man, trusted by all. The firm he left to his son is as robust as an oak."

"But a sapling doesn't always grow true to the parent tree, does it?" Max pressed.

"True enough," Cecil agreed. "Despite being somewhat new to the business, the lad hasn't given us reason to doubt him...yet."

"We must find out everything we can about him—all of them," Rosemary declared. "Someone most certainly knows something that could lead us to the killer."

With crisp determination, her father agreed. "Very well. Henry and I will delve deeper into the investors' backgrounds."

"I'll take charge of the employees," Frederick chimed in. "Keeping everyone calm is key, lest we stir the pot too vigorously and end up with more than just spilled secrets."

"As the wives, Vera and I are in a prime position to engage with the female staff," Evelyn announced, her voice slicing through the air with the precision of a well-aimed dart. "You'd be surprised how much women notice, particularly when they are so often overlooked."

Rosemary watched Max carefully. The last thing he'd want was more civilians involved in his investigation, but he'd been caught off-guard by the matriarch's fervor. Unable to extricate himself from the situation, he paused before nodding respectfully. "Mrs. Woolridge, your involvement is most welcome. A fresh perspective, especially from someone as astute as yourself, could prove invaluable."

Max stood and began gathering his things. "I'm afraid I have to be off again. Please do try to get some sleep. I'll be in touch."

"I'll walk you out." Rosemary ushered Max to the front door, noting how the tightness in his shoulders seemed to extend all the way around his neck and up to clench his jaw firmly.

"I'm sorry, Rosemary," he apologized again when they were out of earshot of the family.

She held up a hand. "You're doing everything you can, Max. We all know that."

He deposited a kiss on her cheek before disappearing into the night.

Once he'd gone, Stella harrumphed indignantly. "Everyone else has an assignment, but what of me? Surely, there's a role I can play."

Evelyn stared at her daughter as if she'd lost her sanity. "Stella, darling, you have young children depending on you."

"So?" Stella retorted, throwing her hands in the air. "What does that matter?"

"There are times when one must think of one's family first, and one's own wants second." Evelyn's voice softened ever so slightly despite the firm undercurrent. "It's selfish to put yourself in harm's way when it's unnecessary. We all must make sacrifices for our children."

"I'm hardly suggesting anything dangerous, Mother, and furthermore, what sacrifices were you forced to make for us?" The words fell out of Stella's mouth before she could stop them.

"My dreams took second place to raising a family. It was not merely a choice; it was my duty." Evelyn's composure wavered just a fraction, but Stella's impatience merely blossomed into annoyance.

"What dreams?" she scoffed, eliciting a sharp look from her father.

"Your mother was a very talented dancer, don't forget," Cecil said proudly, gazing at his wife. She was a member of the Covent Garden Ballet. But she gave it all up when Lionel came along."

Vera turned to peer at Evelyn, the corners of her lips curling with admiration. "The Covent Garden Ballet is rather prestigious."

"Indeed," Evelyn acknowledged with a nostalgic tilt of her head, the memories dancing in her eyes long enough for Rosemary to perceive the faintest flicker of a life once lived in the limelight. "But let us not dwell on the past; we have a present mystery to unravel."

"You lot do, anyway," Stella sulked.

"And a Christmas dinner to plan, don't forget," Frederick added.

"Splendid," Rosemary said, suddenly wary as the reality of putting on Christmas with little help and a lot of her mother began to sink in. Given Evelyn's propensity for wanting things just so and Vera's utter lack of regard for the same, this holiday might go down in the annals of history as the most disastrous one ever.

SEVEN

A thick fog shrouded the city the following morning as Rosemary trailed behind the rest of her family into the Woolridge & Sons offices. Behind the heavy glass doors, the cheerful buzz of conversation and the clatter of typewriters posed a stark contrast to the family's somber mood.

Breaking away from the ladies, Cecil hurried over to where Henry stood near the reception booth. Frederick gave Vera a peck on the cheek before following at his heels.

"Father runs a tight ship," Stella noted, her curiosity piqued by the focused energy of the office around them.

"Indeed, he does," Evelyn replied with a proud nod, her gaze fixed on her husband's slumped shoulders. "I don't envy him the task of breaking the news about Charles."

More than an excuse to plumb for clues to Charles's murder, the ladies' presence was a show of solidarity. One Miranda evidently didn't feel inclined to join, Rosemary realized with disappointment when a thorough search of the room failed to reveal her cousin's presence.

"May I have everyone's attention, please?" Cecil's voice, laden with uncharacteristic heaviness, cut through the clatter of typewriters, drawing the attention of the bustling workers.

The employees swiveled in their chairs, curiosity mingling with unease, only to be met with the gravity of Cecil's somber expression. All chatter ceased as they gathered in the open spaces between rows of desks, concern-filled eyes turned towards their employer.

Cecil cleared his throat, "Dear friends and employees," he began, his voice steady but weighed down with sorrow, "it is with great sadness that I must inform you of the untimely passing of our dear friend and esteemed colleague, Charles Harrington."

Murmurs of shock and grief filled the room, followed by a collective gasp when Cecil revealed the cause of death. "Unfortunately, it seems that Charles was...murdered."

Faces blanched white as parchment, and Lois's hand flew to her mouth to stifle a sob while others exchanged bewildered glances, seeking silent solace in shared disbelief. Rosemary carefully observed the reactions, noting the genuine shock that creased the brows of the clerks and stenographers alike.

Charismatic, always-cheerful Charles had been snatched from their midst without warning. It was unthinkable.

"Given the grave circumstances, tomorrow's charity event must unfortunately be canceled," Cecil continued. "The factory—including the courtyard—is now a crime scene, and we've no choice but to respect the ongoing investigation."

A murmur of disappointment swelled among the staff, and Rosemary felt her mother stiffen beside her, as taut as a finely tuned violin string.

"Finding out who is responsible for this violent act is the utmost priority," Cecil continued. "Charles was a private man, but if any of you know anything about his life that might explain why someone would want him dead, please contact Chief Inspector Whittington of the London police."

As his voice faltered to a close, the office sank into a funereal hush, the air thick with sorrow. But before the silence could take root, it was briskly swept aside by the rustle of Evelyn's skirts as she stepped forward.

"Canceling the charity event is out of the question," she declared, her tone leaving no room for argument. Her gaze swept over the gathered employees. "Think of the children and the families in Clerkenwell. They depend on those donations. Canceling means turning our backs on families who need us."

The office staff, momentarily stunned into stillness, began to stir. Murmurs of assent bubbled up, and heads nodded in agreement. Cecil shot a look of quiet pride towards his wife. Caught between exasperation and admiration, Henry's mouth twitched.

"But wherever will we hold it, Evelyn?" he asked. "Is it even possible to move venues at this juncture? It's twenty-four hours away, after all."

"Perhaps we could make use of the top floor here?" suggested Vera, pointing skyward.

Frederick raised an eyebrow and exchanged glances with his father and uncle.

"It's certainly spacious enough," Cecil said, nodding thoughtfully.

"How?" Henry frowned. "It hasn't been renovated yet."

Vera waved away the comment, a smile playing at the corner of her lips. "Even in its current state, it's a step up from the factory courtyard. We can use the decorations purchased for the original event and whatever else we can get our hands on. When the children see the tree, they won't notice what the walls look like, and the parents will only see happy, smiling faces."

"Then it's settled," Evelyn said, a smile playing at the corners of her lips. "We shall transform the top floor into a winter wonderland for the children."

Rosemary felt the air shift and watched, delighted, as the

collective energy of the office surged with purpose. Relieved to shed the mantle of somber news and don instead the garb of action and goodwill, the staff seemed to breathe easier.

"Your Christmas spirit does the family proud, and I believe this is just what Charles would have wanted," Cecil declared. "As tradition dictates, we must have a Santa Claus to ho-ho-ho for the children. Henry, would you be so kind as to don the red suit once more?"

Henry, whose expression had lost some of its grave lines, nodded with a gentle smile. "Of course, Cecil. Keeping the merriment alive for the little ones would be an honor."

"Splendid," Evelyn clapped her hands once, claiming control of the room. "Everyone, we have an event to save and scant hours to do so. Let's start by scavenging all the decorations we can find. I'm thinking garlands, ribbons, and enough tinsel to make the stars jealous."

As she listened to her mother's grand plans, Rosemary envisioned the countless tasks required to transform the top floor, long neglected and in dire need of renovation, into a space worthy of the Christmas spirit. Truly, it would take a herculean effort to pull it together in such a short time.

Evelyn, however, was undeterred by the monumental undertaking. Accustomed to having a small army of servants at her disposal, ready to jump into action at a moment's notice, she moved through the office with a regal air, her confidence unwavering as she took charge and delegated tasks.

"Stella, my dear, you shall work with Lois on the invitations. It's too late to send corrections, but there are other ways to get the word out. Ring as many people as possible and ask them to pass the news along."

Stella's face momentarily betrayed her annoyance—a crease between her brows that she quickly smoothed over. "Of course,

Mother," she replied, her voice dripping with honeyed acquiescence, gliding towards Lois with a smile so practiced only someone who knew her well would suspect she wasn't quite delighted.

Once all the tasks had been accepted and plans set into motion, Evelyn caught sight of Henry, who stood somewhat apart, his countenance clouded by the day's grim tidings. Excusing herself from the group, she approached her brother-in-law and laid a comforting hand on his shoulder.

"Dear Henry," Evelyn began, her voice filled with genuine concern. "I cannot express how deeply saddened we are by the loss of Charles."

"Yes, well," Henry replied, softening under Evelyn's empathetic gaze. "he was an integral part of our Woolridge & Sons family and will be sorely missed." He offered a tight-lipped smile.

"And speaking of family," she pressed, "how is Miranda? Will we see her today?"

"Miranda will be around soon, I expect." He looked around vaguely, though Rosemary was quite certain he hadn't a clue when his daughter planned to arrive.

"Such a tragedy right before Christmas," Evelyn continued. "But you've always been the resilient sort, haven't you? Stepping in as Santa Claus once more, rallying the troops—It's no wonder Cecil thinks so highly of you. We all do."

"Thank you, Evelyn. Your words mean a great deal."

Rosemary had to admit, albeit grudgingly, that her mother's ability to make others feel seen and valued—when it served her purposes—was nothing short of artful. Her suggestion of Cecil's praise was enough to buoy Henry's spirits, igniting a spark behind his weary eyes. "A dreadful business, this murder. Charles seemed like such a nice man."

"He was. Truly, it doesn't make any sense," Henry insisted, his hands clasped behind his back as if to anchor himself amidst the sea of grief and confusion. "Charles was the perfect choice to lead our American endeavors. Everyone held him in high regard."

"That's what everyone says, but it mustn't be true, must it? For all the affection directed his way, someone bore ill will towards Charles for him to have ended up...well, dead."

The sunlight streaming through the office windows cast Henry's features in sharp relief. Rosemary watched his face closely as he spoke. "You make a fair point, Evelyn," he said with a nonchalance that felt a tad too polished. "But alas, I'm at a loss myself. I can't say I knew of any enemies Charles might have had. As I said, everyone thought highly of him by all accounts."

Evelyn reached out to touch Henry's arm, her fingers shaking slightly. "They say the same about Cecil, don't they? I worry this is more than a mere acquaintance bearing a grudge, but perhaps someone cloaked in the guise of an ally or confidant. You will look after your younger brother, won't you, Henry?"

Before she could prod further, the click-clack of hurried footsteps announced the return of Stella and Lois, accompanied by Thomas Abernathy and Sam Drakeford.

"Ah, gentlemen," Cecil greeted the men, extending a hand. "Please forgive our festive flurry. Grave matters, you understand."

"Of course," Drakeford replied, his voice smooth as silk, though his eyes remained sharp as they roved the office floor.

Even Mr. Abernathy peered around with interest. "Whatever is going on here?"

Cecil beamed. "A valiant effort by my lovely wife to save our annual Christmas benefit for the children of Clerkenwell."

Lois stepped forward timidly, a sheaf of papers clutched to her chest. "Mr. Woolridge, sir." Her voice trembled slightly. "I've just received a message from Eleanor Thornton over in Research & Development. She's wondering if it might be possible for her to work from the office building while the police investigate the factory."

Cecil's eyes softened with understanding. "Of course, Lois. Tell Eleanor she's more than welcome to set up shop up on the first floor. We'll see that she has everything she needs to carry on with her work."

Lois nodded, relief washing over her features. "Thank you, sir. I'll let her know right away."

Henry cleared his throat, drawing attention to himself. "Speaking of messages, Lois, I recall you mentioning that a former employee had been quite eager to speak with someone at Woolridge & Sons. Have you managed to sort out who it was?"

A flush crept up Lois's neck, staining her cheeks a delicate pink. She shuffled the papers in her hands, suddenly finding them utterly fascinating. "I'm still working on that, Mr. Woolridge. With all the commotion surrounding the charity event, the messages have been piling up and..." She trailed off, unwilling to voice the specter of Charles's murder aloud.

Henry's brow furrowed, but he nodded in understanding. "Of course, Lois. Take your time. But do let us know as soon as you have any information. And what of that mess behind the reception area?"

Swallowing hard, Lois stuttered, "Well, sir, that's the lost and found bin. I was instructed to sort through it and donate anything unclaimed to charity. Did I do something wrong?" Her wide eyes caused Henry a moment of chagrin.

"Of course not," he said in an attempt at reassurance. "Carry on."

Taking him quite literally, Lois scurried off with the relief of a mouse who had narrowly escaped being trapped.

"Perhaps, gentlemen," Frederick suggested with a diplomatic tilt of his head, "we might find our discussions more fruitful over a hearty lunch away from these walls?"

"An excellent idea," Cecil concurred, clapping a hand on Mr. Abernathy's back and leading him towards the exit. "We'll tell you all about our little fundraiser on the way. A heartwarming tale to lift your spirits after yesterday's tragedy."

When they'd gone, Evelyn turned to Stella, whose pout had not gone unnoticed. Her expression softened slightly. "My apologies, Stella. Your discomfort was not my intent."

"Mother, really, Lois was as conversational as a mute statue," Stella replied with a roll of her eyes, the corners of her mouth hinting at mischief. "But I dare say, it wasn't entirely dull. The rest of the staff has no such self-control."

Evelyn arched an eyebrow, intrigued despite herself. "Is that so? Do tell, darling. What have you learned?"

"First of all," Stella leaned in, "and perhaps it means nothing, but guess who graced the logbook with her presence just last week? None other than Lady Foxworthy."

"Beatrice?" Evelyn's eyebrow arched in surprise.

"Indeed." Stella's grin was nothing short of triumphant. "And wouldn't you know she failed to mention this little visit before?"

"Curiouser and curiouser," Rosemary murmured, "although I hardly think she's capable of attacking Charles, even in a fit of rage."

Vera shook her head emphatically. "Not without mussing

herself, and she wasn't disheveled at all when we caught up to her outside the factory."

"I think we can count her out as a viable suspect," Rosemary agreed.

When nobody objected, Evelyn said slowly, "Beatrice is a dear friend, and I can't imagine she has any direct link to Charles's demise, but her penchant for untimely arrivals does beg the question—why visit and not speak of it?"

It was Rosemary's turn to arch a brow. "You think she could hold one of the threads in this tangled skein."

"Perhaps," Evelyn declared. With a decisive nod, she glanced towards the reception desk. "Nobody adores a good cause as much as Beatrice. I shall extend an invitation for her to assist us with the fundraiser, and while she's here, we'll glean what we can. Two birds, one stone."

Eight

Now that the idea had taken hold of her, Evelyn commandeered several of the office staff to help whip the top floor into shape in time for the charity event. When she saw the state of the floors, her sharp intake of breath echoed through the space.

"It's filthy!" Evelyn exclaimed.

"It's nothing a good sweeping won't cure," Rosemary cut off the tirade she suspected might be coming. "We can drape garlands around these columns to make them look festive."

"The tree should go there," Vera pointed towards the spot between two windows. "With a nice rug in front for the children to sit on while they wait for Santa."

"The perfect spot," Rosemary agreed, then stepped aside to let the three workers with brooms get to work.

"Well, girls," Evelyn announced, her voice echoing slightly in the cavernous space, "we've done all we can here today, and we've quite the shopping expedition ahead of us if we're to orchestrate a Christmas that lives up to the Woolridge standard. Shall we go to Harrods?"

Vera, her attention captured by the prospect of vibrant shops and bustling aisles, ceased appraising the festoons with a critical eye and turned to her mother-in-law. "If I ever answer no to that question, please call a doctor—or perhaps a priest capable of performing an exorcism."

The cheeky comment elicited a dainty snort from Stella,

who had also brightened. "A spot of shopping is just what we need to clear the doldrums."

For once, Rosemary agreed without protest. Even she had to admit that some holiday cheer was in order. It took another twenty minutes to extricate themselves from the preparations and return to the main floor office, where they discovered Miranda, pale as fresh linen and as late as the proverbial white rabbit, lingering near the reception booth.

"Miranda! There you are, dear," Evelyn remarked, stepping closer, a thread of concern winding through her tone. "Is everything quite all right? You look positively ghastly."

"Mother," Rosemary chided, "don't be rude."

"It is never rude to speak the truth. Why, just look at her. She hasn't an ounce of color in her face."

"I've survived worse, Aunt Evelyn." Miranda swallowed hard and tried to plaster a smile on her face. Even though the rest of her was neat as a pin, her eyes were red-rimmed and distant.

Rosemary's heart went out to her cousin. "No matter how many times I'm confronted with death, it never gets any easier," she said with a gentle sincerity that seemed to surprise Miranda.

Sighing as if Rosemary's gentle tone had unlocked something inside her, Miranda admitted, "I can't shake the image of poor Charles lying there...so still." Her words hung heavy in the air, laden with a misery that threatened to shatter the fragile mood.

"You poor thing," Evelyn fussed. "Perhaps an afternoon at the shops might distract your thoughts? You know how the lights sparkle this time of year. We're headed to Harrods now. Why don't you join us?"

A shadow of a smile attempted to break through Miranda's

stormy expression. It was faint but there—like the first tentative ray of sunshine after a relentless downpour.

"Come along, Miranda," Rosemary coaxed. "A little holiday hustle and bustle might be just what you need to clear the cobwebs from your mind."

"I suppose the distraction couldn't hurt," Miranda murmured, her eyes reflecting a sliver of guarded gratitude.

"It always works for me."

Vera observed the exchange with a curious tilt of her head, and when Miranda stepped out of earshot to gather her things, Rosemary noticed Stella wore a similar expression.

"What?" she asked when they giggled in unison.

Stella shook her head firmly. "Nothing at all." Vera, however, possessed no such restraint.

"That was simply a rare show of diplomacy."

Rosemary slapped a hand over her heart as if wounded. "Are you accusing me of being insensitive?"

"Normally, no, but you must admit, Rosie—you and Miranda getting along is as rare as a summer snowfall. Usually, you're at each other's throats."

"And you find the notion amusing?" Rosemary's hands landed on her hips with mock seriousness. "Shouldn't you be congratulating me for thinking of the welfare of others and aspiring to become a better person?"

Evelyn summoned them before either woman could offer a cheeky retort. "The cab is here, girls." Then she grumbled. "I swear that girl cannot do anything right. I told her to call Whites so we could ride in a nice Citroën. Who does she call? Blacks horse drawn."

"I like the horses," Rosemary said, attempting to diffuse the situation.

Wrapped in their winter finery, the five women stepped out

into the crisp afternoon. As they strolled through the bustling city streets, a cool winter breeze nipped at Rosemary's cheeks, carrying the scent of roasting chestnuts and pine. At Harrods, towering Christmas trees dripped with a dizzying array of baubles in vibrant jewel tones. The iconic department store was a sight to behold, every inch adorned with glittering garlands.

Evelyn's voice cut through the festive din. "Shall we find something special for the children first?"

Momentarily taken aback at being offered any choice at all, Rosemary and Stella merely gaped at their mother.

"Yes, let's," Vera answered brightly, jabbing each of them in the ribs with the sharp points of her elbows.

Rosemary resisted the urge to retaliate, following obediently as Evelyn navigated the crowded aisles with a commanding grace, procuring toys by the dozen for the charity event. Her voice was firm yet laced with honey when she addressed the shop attendants, who scurried about, eager to please.

Despite being earned in humble Pardington, Evelyn's social currency still held sway over the bustling London shopkeepers, her influence just as potent in the city's heart as in the countryside. It was a lesson in soft power Rosemary appreciated, even if she often chafed beneath its application.

"Would this not delight a young mind?" Evelyn asked, lifting a wooden puzzle box and examining it critically before offering an approving nod. "We shall take six."

"Of course, Mrs. Woolridge," the clerk said, his pencil flying gleefully across the order pad. Rosemary could practically see the dollar signs in his eyes.

As he hurried off to fulfill Evelyn's request, Miranda's gaze drifted across the aisle, her eyes widening with a flicker of genuine interest. There, nestled among a vibrant array of stuffed bears and board games, sat a display of exquisite porcelain dolls. Their delicate features had been hand-painted with meticulous care, their glossy hair arranged in perfect ringlets, and their dresses crafted from the finest silks and laces.

Miranda stepped closer, drawn to the dolls like a moth to a flame. Her fingertips trailed reverently over their smooth, cold cheeks and silky hair. For a moment, the weight of her grief appeared to lift, replaced by a childlike wonder that softened her features and brought a hint of color back to her pallid complexion.

The memory of Miranda lugging her favorite dolly everywhere she went washed over Rosemary like a waterfall. Miss Emmaline Pettigrew—Miranda insisted the doll be called by her full name—looked eerily like her owner.

However, not everyone shared Miranda's fondness for her inanimate friend. Rosemary glanced at Stella, noting how her sister's brow furrowed, and her lips pressed together in a thin line. It was the same expression she had worn all those years ago whenever her cousin's doll appeared.

"Miranda, dear," Evelyn suggested, "why don't you select a few of these lovely dolls for the children? I'm certain they would become treasured playthings, just as yours was to you."

Miranda's eyes widened, a flicker of surprise and gratitude dancing within their depths. "You wouldn't mind?" A genuine smile bloomed on her face, chasing away the shadows of grief that had clung to her like a shroud.

"Of course not. Every child deserves a special friend to confide in and cherish. These dolls are simply enchanting, and I can think of no better person to choose them than you."

While Vera joined Evelyn and Miranda, Rosemary deftly steered her sister towards the toy lorries.

"Thank you," Stella said when they were a safe distance away. "Mother seems...different today, doesn't she?"

"Perhaps the Christmas spirit has finally thawed her usual frost," Rosemary mused, her lips quirking upward. She knew better than to take the sudden warmth at face value—her mother was as calculating as she was caring. Yet, as they ventured into the crowd of shoppers, filled with laughter and the scent of roasted chestnuts, even the most cynical heart could be forgiven for believing in seasonal miracles.

The shrill blast of a model train whistle pierced the air, conjuring another flood of childhood Christmas memories for Rosemary: she and Stella cuddled up warm and cozy in front of the fire with their mother; their father huddled around an elaborate train set on the floor with his sons; Frederick and Lionel in cahoots for once—a rarity in those times, when every exchange between brothers consisted of arguing or roughhousing.

The bittersweet recollection threatened to bring tears to Rosemary's eyes.

"Well, well, well, look who we have here!" She was grateful when a familiar voice cut through her reverie, her spirits lifting before she even laid eyes on its source.

Dashing as ever with his roguish smile, Frederick's old school chum, Desmond Cooper, stood poised by the train sets against a backdrop of miniature locomotives chugging along their tiny tracks. He winked and made a beeline towards her, his dapper figure cutting through the hustle with a confident stride.

"So, Rosie, how've you been faring?" Desmond asked after lifting her off the floor in an exuberant gesture she didn't even attempt to curtail. His easy laughter and the twinkle in his eye made the weight of her troubles seem a touch less heavy—even if only for a moment.

"Quite well, Desmond," she replied, straightening her jumper at the same time Stella, who had been admiring a particularly ornate bauble on a nearby display, returned and pointed out, "Although, we seem to be embroiled in another peculiar adventure."

Desmond cocked an eyebrow with a mischievous tilt, his eyes glinting with unspoken jest. "Not another murder? It can't be."

Rosemary grimaced. "One would think such poor luck an impossibility, but one would be wrong. Indeed, we seem to have found ourselves embroiled in yet another death under suspicious circumstances."

"You certainly have committed to a theme, Rosie."

She couldn't help but chuckle at the double entendre, knowing full well Desmond also referred to her pattern of falling for men involved in law enforcement. "I'm not convinced I have much say in the matter if I'm being honest."

"Don't think like that," Desmond said with a grin. "Unraveling mysteries suits you."

"Perhaps it does," Rosemary conceded. Before she could ask him how he'd been faring since they last met, she caught sight of her mother heading their way.

As Evelyn approached, Desmond stepped forward and placed a gentlemanly kiss on her cheek. "Mrs. Woolridge, you look positively radiant today," he said, his voice warm and sincere. "The holiday season certainly agrees with you."

"Desmond, you devil," Evelyn's lips curved in maternal amusement. "Where did you come from? What sort of mischief have you been up to?"

"Oh, you know me, Mrs. Woolridge. I've been gallivanting

about, causing all sorts of delightful chaos. Why, just the other day, I found myself in rather a precarious situation involving a stolen bicycle and a flock of geese. But I managed to charm my way out of trouble, as I always do."

Vera, who had been listening to the exchange with an amused smirk, sauntered up behind Desmond and draped an arm over his shoulder. "I've always said your charms were for the birds," she drawled, her voice dripping with sarcasm. "It's nice to hear you've finally owned up to it."

Desmond spun around and clutched his chest in mock offense, his eyes wide with feigned hurt. "Vera, you wound me! And here I thought we were the best of friends. I'll have you know that my charm is universally acknowledged and appreciated. Speaking of which." he straightened up and pressed past Vera as if she wasn't there, his gaze locked on a new quarry.

"Miranda Woolridge, as I live and breathe." Desmond extended a hand. "It's been an age since we last crossed paths."

"Ah, hello," Miranda said, her voice flat, lacking the girlish enthusiasm that once crackled like static electricity in his presence.

Desmond's brow furrowed slightly at Miranda's lackluster response, but he quickly recovered, his smile never wavering. "I've just returned from a trip to the States. New York City is a marvel, truly. You used to be quite the Americophile, if I remember correctly."

Brow knit with confusion, Rosemary watched Desmond's attempts to charm Miranda evaporate like mist—unseen, unfelt, leaving no trace. Where her young heart had once battled her cousin's over his attentions, now, when the field was open, Miranda only nodded politely, her eyes remaining distant.

"Perhaps you'd have more luck among the pigeons, Des," Vera suggested.

Never one to wallow long, Desmond shrugged off the barb as well as Miranda's snub. "Be sure to keep your wits about you then," he advised Rosemary with a playful wag of his finger before tipping his hat with a flourish and disappearing into the stream of passersby.

After he'd gone, Rosemary's gaze lingered on her cousin. Miranda's patently dismissive response to Desmond simply made no sense. Desmond's fleeting favor—a prize coveted by them both during the first blush of youthful interest, yet ultimately won by neither—had sparked something of a battle resulting in betrayal on Miranda's part.

No matter how much Rosemary might have coveted the young man's attention, she would never resort to tattling on her cousin. Miranda had suffered from no such scruple and had taken great pleasure in whispering the news of a youthful indiscretion into Evelyn's ear, which resulted in Rosemary being scolded at length by her mother. Needless to say, Miranda hadn't been among Rosemary's favorite people—then or now.

That for a time, Rosemary had commanded Desmond's attention felt like less of a victory than it once might have done. Was it possible that all the years of tension between them had simply been the ripples from a pebble thrown into the pond of their childhood?

Perhaps so.

Suddenly, the old rivalry seemed trivial, like a play put on by children who had grown too old for their costumes, and Rosemary realized she couldn't continue to blame the nature of their relationship entirely on her cousin.

"Miranda, you must try this bonbon; it's positively divine,"

Rosemary offered, handing over a chocolate sample a cheery vendor had pressed into her hand moments earlier.

Miranda accepted the sweet with a weak smile. "Thank you," she murmured, biting into it and closing her eyes as if to savor a brief escape from reality.

"If there's anything capable of making a bleak day brighter, it's chocolate," Rosemary declared, hoping to coax a more genuine smile from her cousin. It almost worked, and Miranda's features softened for the first time all afternoon.

"Are we nearly done with our list?" she asked, her tone lighter than before.

"Nearly," Rosemary replied, "but I do believe the best discoveries are often made when one isn't searching for anything at all."

"Come now," Evelyn called out, her tone brooking no argument. "Let's not dilly-dally. We have a great deal to do before evening falls. In fact," her eyes lit with sudden inspiration, and she turned to Miranda, "My dear, why don't you and Henry join us this evening to help decorate the Christmas tree? It's always such a joy to have extra hands, and I'm certain it would do wonders for your spirits."

Miranda's lips curved into a small but sincere smile. "That's very kind of you, Aunt Evelyn. I'm sure Father would be delighted. He's always loved the holiday season."

"Splendid! We'll make an evening of it. You, too, Rosemary. Pop over to Vera and Frederick's house for dinner, won't you? We can trim the tree and perhaps indulge in some mulled wine."

Hearing the invitation issued by someone other than herself, Vera quirked an exquisitely plucked eyebrow. Losing control of her household shouldn't have come as a surprise since Evelyn was notorious for taking over.

Still, Rosemary groaned internally at the thought of preparing a meal with her mother. Evelyn's culinary endeavors were few but legendary—and not in a good way. There was a reason Cecil employed a cook. Rosemary had a feeling it was going to be a long night.

As they resumed their course along the frost-kissed cobblestones of London, the conversation naturally gravitated back to the case of Charles's murder.

"Who stands to gain from Charles's untimely demise?" Rosemary mused, her thoughts weaving through the tangled web of motives and alibis. "Could it be one of the potential investors, or perhaps a disgruntled factory worker looking for retribution? Or what about a colleague acting out of spite or jealousy over his recent promotion? The trouble is, the only time people willfully refrain from speaking ill of the dead is during a murder investigation."

Vera smirked at the observation, but when Rosemary glanced at Miranda, she noticed a flicker of discomfort in her cousin's eyes.

Evelyn was the first to comment. "Employee satisfaction is Frederick's department, and by all accounts, morale is high. The factory is well-maintained, and the workers earn a competitive wage."

Now serious, Vera peered at her mother-in-law with interest. "You're quite well-informed, aren't you?"

"It's part of my duty as a Woolridge wife, isn't it?" Evelyn didn't wait for Vera to answer before adding, "I'd start with the investors; they're both rather shadowy figures."

"Abernathy, perhaps, but Drakeford seems transparent enough."

Miranda let out a sharp breath. "He's certainly that—you

can see right through to the utter cad at his core." Her eyes widened as if she hadn't intended to say as much.

"Agreed," Vera and Rosemary said in unison.

"If you ask me, the motive must be something personal." Stella's smug tone drew four curious pairs of eyes before turning conspiratorial. "You see when Mother saddled me with Lois earlier, I discovered our dearly departed Charles was quite the heartthrob around the office.

Evelyn shrugged. "Well, I suppose it's not surprising. He was a handsome man and quite charming besides. I can see why the ladies might have been drawn to him."

"The ladies in the office positively swooned over him," Stella continued. "You should have seen their faces when they found out he'd been murdered—you'd think the King himself had died!"

"She's right," Vera confirmed. "Charles had a way about him. You would have only needed to visit the office once to notice the flutter of batting eyelashes whenever he passed by— and yet, for all his charm and good looks, he was entirely oblivious. It would have been comical if it wasn't slightly sad."

"Perhaps none of them held his fancy. After all, he spent more of his time at the factory than at the office," Rosemary pointed out. "Though I'll admit, it's not exactly the place for a blossoming romance, considering the scarcity of women in that particular milieu."

"True, true," Evelyn conceded, her gaze drifting momentarily to the festive shop windows. "If we're speaking of potential entanglements, Eleanor Thornton seems a likely choice given the way they were thrown together."

"Precisely." A mischievous grin played across Stella's lips as she twirled a lock of hair around her finger. "It seems the girls in the office were all jealous of Eleanor for working so closely with

Charles. Can you imagine? Spending day after day in that dreary little factory, surrounded by bolts of fabric and the hum of sewing machines, just to bask in his presence?"

Miranda let out a noise somewhere between a laugh and a grunt. "I'd wager Eleanor's ambitions are aimed higher than attracting a man. As I understand it, Mr. Harrington considered her contributions to the Research & Development team quite significant."

Rosemary caught the undertone in Miranda's voice—a blend of admiration and something more guarded. "Significant, you say?" she probed gently.

"Quite," Miranda replied, her gaze darting away. "But of course, I'm hopeless at recalling the details. If you want specifics, you'd have to ask one of the men—or perhaps Aunt Evelyn."

NINE

Later, draped in a kitchen apron and merrily wielding a paring knife, Rosemary gouged the eyes out of a potato with unexpected satisfaction. She added the naked spud to the growing pile in the center of the worktop, noticing her mother's contributions were significantly smaller and more misshapen than her own.

"You want to try to peel rather than slice," Vera explained after observing Evelyn's clumsy command of the blade.

Evelyn's eyebrows, which had been knit together in concentration, abruptly shot to her hairline just as Dash bounded in through the kitchen door. It swung to and fro on its hinges, the sounds of laughter wafting in from the adjacent sitting room where Cecil and Frederick could be seen unpacking the old train set they'd fetched from the attic at Rosemary's suggestion.

Their good humor brought a smile to Rosemary's lips, though it was tempered by the annoyance she sensed in her mother's tight expression. Earlier, Frederick had made a jest regarding Evelyn being out of her element in the kitchen—one Cecil had found a bit too amusing. He'd then unwittingly worsened the situation by failing to realize his error and smooth his wife's ruffled feathers.

"Hold it like this," Vera guided Evelyn's hands, demonstrating the proper technique, "and press your thumb against the potato to stabilize the knife. Then carefully scrape away the peel."

Rosemary had expected her mother to bristle at being taught such a basic skill by her daughter-in-law, particularly when her nerves were already stretched thin. Instead, Evelyn's eyes were attentive and determined.

"I'm simply trying to concentrate on not losing a finger."

"Well, we wouldn't want that now, would we?" Vera laughed, her own knife flashing skillfully through a cut of meat. "I think we've quite enough potatoes, anyway," she added mercifully.

"Thank you, Vera," Evelyn murmured, her voice soft and sincere.

The exchange left Rosemary with a twinge of guilt for her earlier judgments about her mother. Perhaps she'd been wrong to consider Evelyn unbending and unyielding; maybe she was more adaptable than Rosemary realized. While she considered the notion, the expression of incredulity on Vera's face when she'd been kind to Miranda swam in front of Rosemary's eyes, the jest about the priest playing through her mind on a loop.

Rosemary couldn't help but wonder—was *she* the monster who needed to be exorcised?

Vera's voice cut through her self-flagellation. "Right, then," she announced, clapping her hands together after chopping through the last of the carrots. "Time to get everything cooking."

As the ladies bustled around the kitchen, where pots and pans clanged and sizzled, delicious aromas filled the air. Rosemary felt a sense of camaraderie growing between them, fueled by their shared determination to make the evening successful.

"Dinner is served," Vera finally declared, surveying their handiwork.

The meal may not have been the most visually appealing,

with its haphazardly arranged vegetables and slightly over-cooked meat, but it was edible. As they carried the dishes through to the dining room, Vera shot a glance at her fellow cooks and, in a threatening tone, warned her husband and father, "If either of you dare to comment negatively on our culinary skills, I shall personally see to it that you suffer a fate even worse than death."

"Vera!" Rosemary chided, half-shocked and half-amused by her friend's dark humor in the wake of actual tragedy.

"Relax, Rosie," Vera chuckled, giving her a playful nudge. "I'm only joking. Mostly."

Cecil eyed the spread dubiously but merely asked, "Shouldn't we wait for Max?"

"That depends," Frederick replied, eyes glinting mischievously, "on whether Rosie warned him who would be handling the pots and pans."

Later, nestled in the sitting room surrounded by all the people she loved, Rosemary felt lighter than she had in days. Lively banter flowed as freely as the drinks, and the palpable sense of unease that had been present since the discovery of Charles's murder dissolved amidst the laughter and tinsel.

As Rosemary's gaze roved around the sitting room, she couldn't help but feel a twinge of envy for her brother and sister-in-law's home. The Victorian exterior, a stunning example of the era's architectural elegance, remained untouched, while the newly renovated interior boasted sleek lines and bright, open spaces—much larger than her townhouse around the corner, a stark contrast from the dark, ornate chambers of the Woolridge country home.

In other words, as far away from her mother's perfect cup of tea as cold black coffee.

"Frederick, my love, do be careful with that glass ornament!" Vera called out playfully from her perch on the sofa, where she cradled a delicate flute of champagne in one hand. "Your enthusiasm is charming, but I'd rather not have shards of glass adorning the new carpet."

He grinned sheepishly as he carefully hung the fragile ornament, cheeks flushed with exertion and the excess of mulled wine with which he'd washed down his dinner. "My apologies, dearest. I'll endeavor to be more cautious," Frederick promised with mock solemnity.

"See that you do," Vera teased, grinning even as she sipped her champagne. She watched her husband with affectionate amusement, allowing her attention to wander over to where her father-in-law carefully wrapped a garland of strung popcorn around the tree.

"Frederick truly is an accommodating husband," she mused aloud. "I have you to thank for that, don't I, Cecil?"

His gaze slid towards his wife, and Evelyn thawed somewhat under the glow of his admiration. "I can't take all the credit," he admitted modestly. "But I did try to instill in him the importance of keeping his wife happy. It seems to have paid off."

Amid the festive clamor, Rosemary's gaze settled on her Uncle Henry, noting the clouded expression in his eyes. The mulled wine hadn't washed away all the sadness in the room.

Such a pity, she thought as she observed him longingly watch Cecil and Evelyn exchange affectionate glances. It struck her that he seemed envious of his brother's happy marriage—an emotion that hovered heavy over him like a shroud. Miranda also watched her father with sympathy, and Rosemary realized she, too, must be aware of the tender heartache hidden beneath Henry's stoic facade.

Trying to offer some semblance of comfort, she reached over and gently squeezed her cousin's hand in a gesture of solidarity. Miranda didn't recoil or sneer, a sure sign of progress that warmed Rosemary's heart—until Max approached and reached for her hand, pulling her to her feet.

"May I just say that you look lovely this evening?" he said gallantly, widening Rosemary's smile even further.

Miranda's, however, faltered, her eyes darkening as she witnessed the exchange. She raised her glass in a silent toast, drained its contents, and then wobbled back to the drinks trolley for a refill.

Deciding there wasn't much she could do for Miranda, Rosemary barred the worry from her mind and, finding herself positioned beneath the mistletoe, allowed herself to be caught up in the moment with Max. It didn't last long before Frederick tapped him on the shoulder. "If you're quite through manhandling my sister, we could use some help mounting the star," he said, winking over his shoulder as he pulled Max away, "Just doing my brotherly duty."

A low murmur of heated words broke through the laughter and clinking glasses to capture Rosemary's attention. The flickering fire cast its warm glow upon the cold faces of Evelyn and Stella as an argument unfolded between them.

"Darling, I merely said that Vera's choice of wallpaper is delightful," Evelyn remarked, a trace of annoyance in her voice. "I don't see why you're making such a fuss."

"Because when I suggested using the same pattern at home, you called it gauche!" Stella snapped, her fingers nervously twisting the hem of her dress. "It's as if you'll heap praise anyone but me."

"Oh, for goodness sake."

"Stella, surely that's not true," Rosemary interjected gently, trying to diffuse the situation. "Mother's tastes may have changed since then. We all evolve over time." It sounded unlikely, even to her, but she pasted an encouraging smile on her face.

"Exactly, my dear." Evelyn's tone was regal and dismissive. "People can change their minds. There's no need to take it personally, Stella."

Despite their efforts, Stella's irritation only intensified. Anger flushed her cheeks and pursed her lips into a pout that Rosemary remembered quite well from her youth. It was the one that usually preceded a five-alarm temper tantrum. Even though they weren't children anymore, she knew Stella was still quite capable of incurring their mother's wrath—and that, she was confident, would put a nail in the coffin of the festive mood.

The men huddled together on the other side of the coffee table, their voices low and somber as they discussed Charles's murder. Eager to redirect her sister's attention from her wounded pride, Rosemary used the topic as an opportunity.

"Stella, why don't you tell Father what you learned about Mr. Harrington earlier today."

Her expression cleared, and Stella needed no further prompting. "Well," she said hesitantly, her voice barely audible, "Lois told me he was well-liked, though nobody seemed to know much about him."

"Curious, isn't it?" Rosemary mused, observing the room. Her gaze landed on Miranda, who had succumbed to the warmth and comfort of the settee, her breathing slow and even as she cuddled with Dash. The sight brought a fleeting smile to

Rosemary's lips, the small moment of innocence a salve against the chaos that enveloped them.

Henry, fidgeting with his cuff links, interjected softly, "I must admit, I didn't know much about Charles's personal life either." He shifted his attention to Frederick. "How are you faring with his files?"

Frederick's eyes were serious as he responded, "I'm working through them, but there's a great deal to interpret. The last six months have been an absolute disaster. Finding someone competent to prepare the reports for R&D must be prioritized in the new year. I hate to say it, but someone at least half as diligent as Palmer."

"Wait," Stella interrupted, her irritation with her mother forgotten. "Do you mean Johnathan Palmer?"

"Stella, darling, how do you know that name?" Cecil asked, his voice laced with curiosity.

"I saw it scribbled on one of the message pads on Lois's desk," Stella explained. "Why? Is it important?"

"Palmer used to work in R&D," Cecil said, addressing Max directly as he divulged the information. "Charles fired him months ago, and we haven't heard from him since."

He looked at Henry, who stared blankly at the glass in his hand before coming to himself and nodding in agreement. "Hide nor hair."

"Until now, it seems," Max mused, his eyes narrowing as he pondered the implications. "Why do you think he'd reach out after all this time?"

"Perhaps he knows something," Rosemary offered cautiously, her mind racing with possibilities. "Something that could shed light on Charles's murder or the predicament left by his passing."

"Or maybe he's involved himself," Henry added darkly, the

lines around his eyes deepening as suspicion took hold. "We mustn't rule anything out. Palmer was certainly angry with Charles."

Cecil turned to Max again. "I trust you'll look into this matter?"

"Of course, Mr. Woolridge," Max assured him, his jaw set with determination. "I'll see what I can uncover about this Johnathan Palmer and his recent activities."

"Thank you," Cecil replied, the gratitude in his voice tinged with an undercurrent of trepidation that caused Rosemary to shiver involuntarily. Suddenly, she was keenly aware of the fragility of their reprieve, recognizing it as the same sort of giddy, mistaken relief often described by people who had been through the eye of a storm.

"Are you all right?" Max asked, noticing her silence and furrowed brow. Even amidst the escalating tension, his concern for her well-being warmed her heart.

"Yes," she answered, attempting a reassuring smile. "Just lost in thought." Her mind raced with possibilities, each more unnerving than the last.

"Promise me you'll be careful, Max," Rosemary implored, her eyes searching his face for reassurance. "We don't know what we're dealing with here, and my intuition insists there's more to Charles' death than meets the eye."

"Rosemary, my dear," Max said softly, his gaze never wavering from hers, "I promise you, I will do everything in my power to protect you and your family. We will get to the bottom of this together. Like we always do."

TEN

By the following day, as promised, the top floor of the Woolridge & Sons office building had been transformed into a holiday daydream. Between a pair of tall windows overlooking a picturesque view of London's snow-dusted skyline towered a massive Christmas tree covered in colorful baubles. Beneath its boughs lay a cornucopia of gifts, each carefully wrapped in red holly-sprigged paper and tied with ribbons, awaiting distribution to the less fortunate children attending the event.

"The doors open in just under an hour," Evelyn announced, eliciting an excited twitter from the room. "Our Santa Claus will make his entrance shortly thereafter."

Dozens of employees, office and factory workers alike, had volunteered to lend a hand. Several had even come fittingly dressed as Santa's elves, proving Rosemary wrong on one count: Evelyn Woolridge didn't require a paid staff to do her bidding. All she needed was a take-charge attitude and the ability to delegate effectively.

Even Eleanor had been coaxed from where she was holed up in her makeshift R&D office, the scent of hot cocoa and candy canes too enticing to ignore. Rosemary wondered if she'd gone home at all the previous night, but she didn't have time to ponder the notion any further when Mr. Abernathy strode in carrying a cardboard box overflowing with red tartan bows.

Lady Foxworthy's gaze drifted from the flower arrangement she'd been meticulously adjusting to exclaim, "Mr. Abernathy! What an unexpected—and pleasant—surprise," her cheeks rosy with a flush that might have been attributed to more than just the room's warmth.

"Ah, but how could I resist such a charming invitation to assist for a worthy cause?" Abernathy replied smoothly, his smile disarming as he rolled up his sleeves and approached a stack of chairs with easy confidence, hoisting them with the air of a man accustomed to labor despite his polished appearance.

Lady Foxworthy practically swooned.

"See that, Rosemary? A true gentleman is never afraid to lend a hand." Her eyes lingered on him with unconcealed admiration.

"Quite right, Beatrice." Rosemary had to bite the corner of her lip to keep from smiling, but Mr. Abernathy made no such effort, grinning roguishly.

"I must say, Lady Foxworthy, I'm impressed to see you here. It's not every day one sees a woman of your stature so eager to get her hands dirty, as it were."

"Mr. Abernathy, you'll find I'm full of surprises." She lobbed the proverbial ball across the net, and he returned it just as effortlessly.

"You are a rare breed, Lady Foxworthy. Your dedication to this cause is truly admirable."

"I find few joys more satisfying than acts in service of a greater good."

"A sentiment with which I couldn't agree more."

Rosemary could almost hear Sam Drakeford's eyes roll from where he leaned against the wall, arms crossed, watching the exchange with ill-concealed amusement. His sullen posture suggested he found the entire affair rather pedestrian—a far cry from Mr. Abernathy, who exuded enthusiastic energy as he shared tales of his philanthropic journeys with an enraptured Lady Foxworthy.

"Why, just last year, I had the privilege of traveling to a remote village in India to assist in constructing a school. The children there, bright-eyed and eager despite the poverty that surrounded them, were positively overjoyed at the prospect of a proper education."

"Saint Abernathy, indeed," Drakeford drawled under his breath.

Mr. Abernathy chuckled, the sound rich and untroubled, as he adjusted his collar. "Ah, young man," he quipped, "as I said before, saints don't enjoy the comforts of establishments like the Grand Lion Hotel."

Rosemary observed the exchange, noting the slight tightening at the corners of Drakeford's mouth—a tell as clear as day. He masked it quickly with another sip of lemonade, but the seed of discord had been sown. As if sensing her attention, he lifted his head, their eyes briefly locking before his skittered away. At least he looked less disheveled today—every inch of him pressed and polished and proper. A point in his favor, Rosemary supposed, given his attitude at the moment.

"The Grand Lion is quite the establishment," Lady Foxworthy interjected, her voice a musical trill that resonated with underlying intent. She arched a perfectly groomed eyebrow at Mr. Abernathy. "It happens to be in my neighborhood."

He turned towards her, his expression shifting to one of pleasant surprise. "Then you must know who owns the house with those exquisite stained glass windows that catch the sunrise. A remarkable sight—they brighten my morning strolls considerably."

If possible, Lady Foxworthy appeared even more besotted than before. "That's my house."

A slow smile spread across Mr. Abernathy's face. "Truly? What an extraordinary coincidence! I must say, your taste in architecture is impeccable. The craftsmanship of those windows is simply unparalleled—the way they transform the light, casting a kaleidoscope of colors across the street... it's positively enchanting. Much like the lady of the house herself, if you'll pardon my boldness."

Pardon my something, Rosemary thought as she considered which of the pair might be the spider, and which the fly.

Lady Foxworthy blushed, her hand fluttering to her chest as if to still her racing heart. "Oh, Mr. Abernathy, you flatter me."

"Flattery implies an embellishment of the truth, Lady Foxworthy. I assure you, my words are sincere." His gaze lingered on her, warm and appreciative. "I don't suppose you'd be willing to share how you acquired the property...perhaps over a drink at the Grand Lion sometime?"

Rosemary mentally put a shilling on Lady Foxworthy saying yes.

Ready to prove her correct, Lady Foxworthy's eyes sparkled with delight at the prospect, but before she could utter a word, Vera called out from across the room where she and Stella were busy hanging garlands. "Mr. Abernathy! Could you lend us a hand? We need a tall, strapping someone to reach the tops of the windows."

"Duty calls," he said, winking at Lady Foxworthy before sauntering away.

Evelyn quickly materialized at her side, wearing an expression of both amusement and concern. "Be careful with that one, Beatrice," she cautioned, her voice low and conspiratorial. "He's as smooth as a polished river stone and just as difficult to grasp."

Lady Foxworthy startled slightly, drawn out of her reverie by Evelyn's words. She turned to face her friend, a faint blush coloring her cheeks. "Oh, Evelyn, don't be such a worrywart. Mr. Abernathy is a perfect gentleman."

Evelyn arched an eyebrow, unconvinced. "A perfect gentleman, perhaps, but one with secrets. No one knows where he came from or how he made his fortune. He's a mystery, Beatrice, and mysteries can be dangerous."

Lady Foxworthy waved a dismissive hand, her bracelets jingling with the motion. "Oh, pish posh, Evelyn. A little mystery never hurt anyone. It adds to his allure, don't you think?" Her eyes drifted back to where Mr. Abernathy was now engaged in straightening garlands, his tall frame stretching to reach the top of the windows. The sunlight filtering through the glass seemed to cast a halo around his dark hair, and Lady Foxworthy sighed wistfully.

"That's easy for you to say, Evelyn. You've found your perfect match. It's rare to find a man who's steady, reliable, devoted...and utterly transparent in his affections for you. Honestly, you don't know how lucky you are to have a man like Cecil." She turned back to her friend, her expression softening. "Not all of us are so fortunate."

Evelyn's brow furrowed, "I do know how lucky I am to have Cecil," she said, her voice approaching a shrill, defensive tone before she swallowed hard and said, "I simply want you to be safe, of course. There's a killer amongst us, after all."

"Surely you can't think Mr. Abernathy had anything to do with Mr. Harrington's murder?" Lady Foxworthy scoffed.

"He's far too likable—and handsome—to be a cold-blooded killer."

"In my experience," Rosemary interjected, "killers are just as likely to be likable—and handsome—than not. Though it does seem a stretch," she added when Lady Foxworthy's lips began to purse into a sour expression. "Whatever motive he might have remains a mystery. Even so, I agree with Mother. Best to keep your guard up, at least until this whole horrid affair is resolved."

"I'll take that under advisement," Lady Foxworthy said vaguely, her gaze still locked on her quarry.

"I do hope Mr. Abernathy is all you believe him to be, Beatrice. Both for your sake and for the company's."

"What do you mean, Evelyn?" Lady Foxworthy's brow creased with concern.

"This whole thing, well, it could spell trouble for Cecil, you know."

"Murder does cast rather a long shadow, doesn't it?"

"It does. Any clue could be the key to solving Charles's murder. Did you happen to see anything interesting when you were here last week?" Evelyn asked innocently, but not innocently enough for her astute friend.

"Taking a page out of your daughter's book and engaging in a bit of amateur sleuthing, are you?" Lady Foxworthy's amusement quickly turned to impatience when Evelyn's eyes remained trained on the flower arrangements. "I came by to drop off my check for the children's benefit if you must know. Surely you don't think I had anything to do with the murder?"

Finally, Evelyn looked up. "Of course not, Beatrice. I merely thought perhaps you'd seen something of import. You do always manage to pick up the most scintillating tidbits."

Somewhat mollified, Lady Foxworthy smiled. "Truer words have never been spoken."

Cecil's voice boomed across the room, cutting through the chatter and rendering moot anything else she might have said. "Go public, you say?"

Rosemary turned just in time to see Sam Drakeford appealing to the Woolridge patriarch with what appeared to be casual interest. "Indeed, Mr. Woolridge. It's the modern way, after all," he said, the suggestion hanging in the air like a challenge.

"The thought has never quite appealed to us," Cecil replied, his polite smile not reaching his eyes.

"Woolridge & Sons could expand even further with the right investment."

"Ah, but we cherish our family roots, you see," Cecil stated firmly, though not unkindly as if reminding everyone of the Woolridge legacy. "Tradition is part of our foundation. Of course, Frederick will have his say when the time comes." He gestured towards his son. "He could certainly take the company public if that's what he felt was best."

At Cecil's side, Henry's expression soured as if the very idea caused him physical discomfort. His hands clenched momentarily before he forced them to relax. Rosemary tilted her head slightly, her gaze lingering on him as she noted the tension rippling beneath his carefully maintained composure. Was it simply the idea of change that ruffled his feathers, or did he resent the faith their father placed in Frederick?

"Change can be a fearsome thing," Mr. Abernathy mused, "but stagnation is worse—a pond choked by its own stillness. Going public is not without its merits. It is possible to retain control and still embrace expansion."

"Public offering?" Frederick moved to his father's side, a

touch of jest in his voice. "I think not. Father has built something more than a business—he's crafted a legacy, a testament to his acumen and steadfast vision. And let us not forget Henry's shrewd financial decisions that have kept us on an even keel through many a storm. We'd be fools to try and rock the boat at this juncture, wouldn't we?"

Henry's expression remained carefully neutral, though his eyes betrayed a flicker of pride at the acknowledgment. Cecil's chest visibly swelled with it.

"That's it, son," he replied with a warmth that spread through the room like the first rays of dawn. "You've grasped the essence of Woolridge & Sons perfectly."

Quite the transformation from rakish schoolboy to devoted family man, Rosemary thought, admiring Frederick's newfound dedication. He'd certainly come a long way from the lad who'd once awakened in a field after a night's drinking.

Mr. Abernathy clapped him on the back. "A fine position, to be sure. I was merely playing the role of devil's advocate. The Woolridge values piqued my interest in this venture—the sense of family and the commitment to quality and innovation. I'm thrilled you've no intention of changing any of it."

Rosemary watched as Sam's eyebrows arched, his lips twitching into a smirk. The man seemed to find joy in withholding his approval as if enthusiasm were a currency too precious to spend.

Evelyn's eyes narrowed ever so slightly, her lips pursing in distaste. "That man irks me," she confessed. "He seems to enjoy stirring up trouble and disappearing once it starts to bubble over."

"Mother, disliking Mr. Drakeford doesn't make him a villain," Rosemary chided gently, a playful smile tugging at the corners of her mouth. "Don't get me wrong, he's undoubtedly a cad—but a spineless one, in my estimation. A dandelion puff blown hither and thither by the slightest breath of challenge."

"Perhaps," Evelyn mused, though unconvinced. "But even a spineless cad can harbor sinister intentions beneath his flimsy veneer."

For once, Rosemary and her mother wholeheartedly agreed.

Eleven

"Have you seen Uncle Henry?" Stella found Rosemary shortly before the doors were slated to open. They'd pulled off a miracle, preparing the event space in less than a day. Now that it was nearly time for the festivities, only a few minor details were left to put into place. "Mother's looking for our jolly old Saint Nick. It's nearly time for his big entrance."

Sincerely doubting there was any merit in further fussing over the distribution of tree ornaments as her mother had commanded, considering the children's eyes would be glued to Santa, his cheerful little elves, and the stacks of gifts beneath its branches, Rosemary linked arms with Stella and abandoned the effort without further prompting.

"I saw Henry head that way with Miranda only moments ago." She pointed to a door at the back of the room, which led to a wide corridor Evelyn had designated for storing decorations until needed.

Rosemary and Stella approached the corridor, their footsteps muffled by the plush carpet runner. As they neared the door, which stood slightly ajar, they could hear the rustle of fabric and the murmur of voices within. They peered around the corner to see Uncle Henry shrugging into his Santa costume with the aid of Miranda and hung back, not wanting to interrupt.

"Truly, it should have been you all along, Father,"

Miranda's voice carried a note of anger tempered with unexpected affection. "I know how much it means to you."

"Ha! To think the opportunity comes knocking once more," Henry chuckled, his voice rich with a sudden sense of purpose.

"A little Christmas miracle," Miranda replied.

Stella's fingers tightened around her arm, and they exchanged a curious glance.

"I do hope so, my dear," Henry replied, his voice slightly muffled. After a moment, he added, "I must admit, this suit is a bit snug around the middle. I fear I may have indulged in one too many mince pies this season."

"Nonsense," Miranda said, her tone warm and reassuring. "You make a most convincing Saint Nicholas, and the suit fits you like a glove. Now, let me help you with the beard."

Henry chuckled, his eyes crinkling at the corners as he gazed at his reflection in the full-length mirror. "I must admit, I feel rather jolly in this getup," he said

"There, your beard is straight, and you look as jolly as you feel," Miranda replied. "I think it's time for your grand entrance."

"You don't think..." Stella said after Henry and Miranda had gone. "Perhaps Uncle Henry wanted Charles's job?"

Rosemary glanced at Stella warily. "It's the sort of theory that would make for thrilling parlor gossip, but it hardly seems plausible. He's a Woolridge, after all. He could have appealed to Father if he'd wanted to head the offices in New York."

"Murder is such a grim business," Stella mused, straightening a crimson ribbon with an artist's touch. "But to think of Uncle Henry driven to such extremes over a job? It's positively Gothic."

Yet, as unexpected as a loose thread in an otherwise neat

weave, Henry's words hung in Rosemary's thoughts. "Even so, keep your ears open. If he does have secrets, they won't stay buried for long."

"Best we keep this flight of fancy to ourselves," Stella agreed, sharing a conspiratorial smile with her sister. "We shouldn't cast aspersions on family, after all."

"Anything to avoid Mother's wrath. Speaking of whom, let's rejoin the others before our absence is noted."

"I," Stella heaved a sigh, "am already on her naughty list. She's somehow decided it is my fault that my husband and children haven't arrived. It seems I am to blame for the traveling conditions between here and Oxford."

"Mother can be difficult when she's in the midst of planning something," Rosemary commiserated, pulling Stella along.

It was easy to get swept up in the joyous tide of goodwill that reached a crescendo as Henry, garbed in crimson and white, emerged from behind a grand velvet curtain with a resounding "Ho, ho, ho!" His voice boomed through the room like the bright peal of church bells on Christmas morning. The children, who had been sipping hot cocoa and nibbling on gingerbread, suddenly abandoned their treats and clustered around the towering figure of Santa Claus.

"Come now, don't be shy!" Henry beckoned with open arms, his eyes twinkling beneath the fluffy brim of his hat. One by one, the little ones approached, some bold and chattering, others bashful but beaming.

Smiling contentedly, Rosemary watched from the edge of the laughter-filled throng. She recalled a distant winter's day when she had slipped on the frozen pond, her knee reddened and smarting. It was Uncle Henry who had found her, scooped her up in his strong arms, and whisked her away to warmth and safety. He had bandaged her wound with such gentleness, telling stories of brave knights and far-off adventures until her tears were dry, and she was ready to embark on make-believe quests once more.

"Santa, may I have a doll?" piped up a little girl with braided hair and hopeful eyes. Rosemary's heart swelled as she witnessed Henry's tender interaction, his hearty laugh echoing as he assured her that Santa would remember.

"I'd say the odds are in your favor. Every child here will find joy under the tree this year," he proclaimed, sending her off with a smile and hoisting a little boy onto his knee. "And what might your wish be, young man?"

Rosemary's doubts about her uncle's innocence dissipated as quickly as they had risen. Still, her relief wouldn't last long, for an unforeseen needle was poised to prick the festive bubble that enclosed the room. A shadow fell across the polished floorboards, drawing Rosemary's gaze to the entrance where Max stood framed in the doorway. His face, which usually bore a charmingly crooked smile, was now etched with gravity.

He did not look like he was there to experience good tidings of great joy.

Rosemary's stomach churned with sudden unease, her intuition sharpening like the point of an arrow. Heart lodged in her throat, she watched Max lean to speak into her father's ear with a hushed urgency. Excusing herself from Stella's side, she approached, the fluttering in her chest intensifying as she drew nearer.

Cecil's face, usually a mask of composure, crumbled into an expression of stark disbelief. His eyes widened, his jaw clenched —a silent tableau of shock that sent a chill across Rosemary's skin. Then, with a fortitude born of necessity, he straightened his shoulders and made his way to where Henry handed out toys to a line of eager children.

The tender moment between Saint Nick and an awestruck child dissolved as Cecil placed a firm hand on Henry's shoulder. "Excuse us," he forced a smile that didn't quite reach his eyes. "Santa needs to step away for a moment."

Henry rose, confusion clouding his expression. "Is something amiss?" he asked, brushing off his plush red coat, the festive fabric now oddly out of place.

"Let's discuss it away from little ears, shall we?" Cecil suggested with a pointed nod towards the children.

"Of course, Mr. Woolridge," Max agreed.

A sympathetic-looking volunteer dressed as an elf in jaunty green caps and candy-striped stockings leaped into action, nearly knocking over Eleanor, who had been standing in the shadows watching. "Who wants to hear a story about Santa's magical reindeer?" she asked brightly, distracting the children while Cecil led Henry and Max into the staging corridor, the rest of the Woolridges trailing behind.

When Lady Foxworthy, joined by Mr. Abernathy and Sam Drakeford, made to accompany the family, Max attempted to halt their intrusion. "Perhaps it's best if we allow Mr. Woolridge to handle this matter privately," he suggested, his tone diplomatically firm.

"Has it occurred to any of you that we who are on the outskirts of this sordid affair might also be in danger?" Drakeford pointed out. "We ought not to be left in the dark."

Cecil, exchanging a glance with his brother, waved a hand. "It's quite all right, Max. He makes a fair point. They were all present for the discovery of Charles's body. It seems they have a right to be involved."

"Very well then."

Henry, his brow furrowed beneath the fluffy brim of his

Santa hat, turned to face Max. "What's this all about, Inspector?"

Max's voice was clear and steady, but he kept it low to avoid causing any more of a scene. "Henry Woolridge, I'm afraid you're under arrest for the murder of Charles Harrington."

A collective gasp swept through the family; even Rosemary felt a jolt despite bracing for the blow. She wanted to refute the claim, but the regret in Max's eyes silenced her before the words could form.

"Murder?" Henry's voice wavered incredulously, his hands rising instinctively as if to ward off the accusation. "This is preposterous!"

"Please come quietly, Mr. Woolridge," Max continued. "We really must sort this out at the station."

Henry stiffened and allowed Max to click the restraints around his wrists. "I wouldn't dream of resisting arrest, Inspector Whittington."

"Everyone, I must apologize for this...disruption." Max addressed the group, but his eyes found Rosemary's among the sea of startled faces. "There wasn't time to warn you."

Her throat tightened, emotions swirling within her chest and knotting into a lump she couldn't quite swallow. His apology, sincere as it was, did little to ease the sting of betrayal gnawing at her insides. It was one thing to chase shadows and unveil secrets with Max by her side, quite another to see him as the harbinger of turmoil within her own family.

Miranda, her cheeks flushed with anger and shock, stepped out of the stairwell, surging forward like a storm about to break. "This is an outrage!" she spat. "He's done nothing wrong! You cannot possibly—"

Even in his moment of duress, Henry managed the silent command that cut through Miranda's fiery protest like a knife through silk. It was the same gesture he had used when they discovered Charles's body—and also years before upon her mother's sudden departure.

Rosemary's heart lurched at the sight, the memory of that day pressing down on her. She recalled Miranda's face then—pale and drawn—now twisted in defiance and resignation. Henry's daughter bit back whatever storm she'd been about to unleash and pressed her lips into a thin line, but her eyes blazed with an inner fire that was far from extinguished.

The crowd parted as Max's constable ushered Henry out, the silence punctuated only by the soft shuffle of feet and the sound of the holiday carols, their joyful tunes clashing with the gravity of the situation. With hearts heavy and minds teeming with questions, the family watched as their Santa was led away into a cold night that no longer held the promise of holiday magic.

Max's expression was solemn beneath the brim of his hat. "Lois came forward," he began, the words heavy with regret. "She claims she saw Henry and Charles engaged in a heated exchange mere days before his death."

Lois's skittish reaction to Henry the previous day when he'd asked her about the telephone messages suddenly made sense to Rosemary, but on the other hand, there hadn't been any tension between Charles and her uncle the morning of the tour. "An argument hardly seemed grounds for arrest," she pointed out.

"True," Max conceded, "but unfortunately, he also has a feasible motive, and I'm afraid the footprint at the scene had been analyzed and found to be his size. Combined, it's enough that I'm duty-bound to act. I wish it were otherwise, truly."

His regret was palpable, but Miranda remained unmoved.

Her face flushed a deep crimson as her hands balled into fists at her sides.

"It's preposterous!" she seethed, eyes fiery with indignation. Without her father's steadying presence, her emotions blazed out of control. "My father, who has weathered storms of both nature and heart, would never succumb to base instincts. He is utterly incapable of such barbarity!"

Eleanor stepped forward, her mouth open as if she wanted to speak, but the sight of Miranda's fiery expression caused her jaw to snap shut, and she stepped back to her place in the shadows.

"Quite so," Lady Foxworthy said, wrapping a protective arm around Miranda. For a moment, Rosemary thought she might flinch away from the contact, but she stood stock still and allowed herself to be fussed over. "Nobody who knows Henry would believe it for one second!"

"You're right," Rosemary interjected, her soothing tone meant to quell her cousin's fire before it raged beyond control, "Uncle Henry is a great many things, but a murderer isn't among them. And yet, Max must do his due diligence. Even you must be able to understand that, Miranda."

"Understand this," her cousin snapped, sharp as a whip crack, "I don't care about your precious inspector's due diligence. I care about my family, which is more than I can say for you."

With that, she spun on her heel and made to follow after her father with a fury that left no room for pursuit.

"Your loyalty is admirable," Mr. Abernathy said, coming to stand next to Lady Foxworthy, whose hands still trembled.

The tension in the room lingered like the remnants of a bitter fog, but Frederick's voice cut through it with ease. "Miranda's fire will die down," he assured them based on the long history shared with his cousin. "Her fuse is short, but she's sensible at heart."

Rosemary nodded, considering Frederick's words. "Perhaps. And if not, we will clear Uncle Henry's name and repair bridges later. Max, how did this happen? And what of the Johnathan Palmer lead?"

"Who is Johnathan Palmer?" Sam Drakeford's voice cut through the murmurs, a note of curiosity sharpening his tone.

"Johnathan Palmer is a former employee," Frederick explained, his words measured. "Unfortunately, his journey with us ended after Charles let him go."

Drakeford's eyes widened as he threw up his hands. "A disgruntled ex-employee? Why didn't you mention any of this before?" he prodded. "And why isn't this Johnathan Palmer the one being arrested?"

"Now let's just calm down, Mr. Drakeford," Max said, his voice strained. "We're doing everything we can to track him down, but given the holidays and the impending storm, it may take a while." Pointedly, he turned away from Drakeford to address Cecil and the rest of the family. "Once Henry's been processed, you'll be able to speak with him. Now, if you'll excuse me, I must be on my way."

As Max turned to leave, Rosemary caught his eye. For a fleeting moment, the mask of professionalism slipped, revealing a mixture of regret and determination. Then, with a curt nod, he strode out of the room, his footsteps echoing in the sudden silence.

Cecil cleared his throat, breaking the spell of silence that had fallen over the room. "I need to go speak with Henry," he announced, his voice steady despite the worry lines etched deeply around his eyes. "Rosemary, I think you ought to come along as well."

Evelyn, who had been uncharacteristically quiet throughout the ordeal, stepped forward. Her usual composure was fractured, revealing a vulnerability Rosemary rarely saw in her mother. "I'm coming too," she declared, her tone brooking no refusal. "He's my brother-in-law, after all."

Frederick, ever the voice of reason, placed a reassuring hand on Evelyn's shoulder. "Of course, you should go," he said gently. "Vera and I will wrap up things up here. We'll make sure the children don't suspect anything amiss."

Evelyn nodded. "Stella, darling, stay and help your brother, won't you?"

It seemed as though Stella might argue for a moment but resisted the urge. "Of course."

As the Woolridges prepared to depart, Lady Foxworthy clasped her jeweled fingers together. "My dears, you simply must allow me to offer you the use of my car," she said, her voice dripping with honeyed concern. "It's far too cold to wait for a taxi, and my driver, Jensen, is an absolute marvel. He knows every street in the city and can navigate through this dreadful weather as though he were born with a steering wheel in his hands."

"That's very kind of you," Cecil said, his voice tinged with gratitude. "We would be most appreciative."

Evelyn hesitated, her brow furrowing with concern. "But Beatrice, how will you get home?"

Lady Foxworthy's lips curved into an enigmatic smile, her eyes twinkling with mischief. "Oh, don't you worry about me, darling. I'm sure I'll manage just fine."

As if on cue, Mr. Abernathy appeared at her elbow. "I'd be more than happy to see Lady Foxworthy safely home."

TWELVE

pon arriving at the station, they were greeted by the sight of Henry, still clad in the costume of Saint Nicholas. The absurdity of his attire—a bright red suit trimmed with white fur—starkly contrasted the drab stone walls around him. His discomfort was palpable; his hands fidgeted with the false beard that lay crumpled on his lap, and his eyes darted like a cornered animal's.

"Good heavens," Cecil murmured, his brow creasing with concern as he beheld his younger brother's plight.

Max, who had been awaiting their arrival, shared none of Cecil's restraint. His voice boomed through the corridor, echoing off the cold, hard surfaces. "This isn't a joke! Get the man some proper clothes," he barked at the constables standing nearby. Flinching at his command, they scrambled to comply, mumbling apologies as they hurried away.

"There's no need to trouble yourselves on my father's account," Miranda's voice cut like a diamond on glass, drawing Rosemary's attention to the woman standing near the door with her fingers curled into fists at her side. The festive spirit that had filled her heart mere hours ago had vanished. She glared back at Rosemary with an intensity that could have melted steel. "You've done quite enough already."

Evelyn tried desperately to catch her niece's eye. She reached out a tentative hand, "Miranda, please..."

But Miranda refused to acknowledge her. She fixed her gaze

on Rosemary until Max interrupted the awkward silence to say, "Your father has requested your presence during questioning, Miss Woolridge. I'm afraid the rest of you will have to wait here."

Miranda followed Max, and after several moments, Rosemary moved to follow Miranda.

"Where are you going?" Evelyn hissed at her daughter. "Max told us to wait here."

"So he did," Rosemary said, ignoring her mother's warning glare. "I want to see if I can hear anything."

Her luck held when she sidled around the corner to find the door of the interrogation room hanging slightly ajar. Careful to remain completely silent, Rosemary positioned herself where she could see and hear but not be seen and settled in for a bout of eavesdropping.

The red suit still clung to Henry's frame as he sat across from Max, who wasted no time addressing the matter at hand. "Mr. Woolridge," he began, eyes fixed upon Henry with a respectful intensity while still demanding the truth. "Why did you not inform us of your disagreement with Charles prior to his untimely death?"

Henry shifted uncomfortably, the plush red fabric rustling under the scrutiny. "I had presumed—" He swallowed hard, his voice strained, "Bringing it up...I feared it might cast unnecessary suspicion my way."

"Unnecessary, Mr. Woolridge?" Max's tone sharpened to a razor's edge. "Might I remind you that your alibi is less than airtight? Given the current predicament, surely you can see how failing to divulge such a matter might appear to those of us seeking justice. How it might be construed as evasion, or worse?"

The accusation hung in the air, weighty and unyielding.

Henry's hands shook as he tugged at the faux fur trim of his coat. He looked every bit the cornered man.

"Who among us hasn't quarreled the workplace? Woolridge & Sons is no small enterprise; it has its share of tensions and disagreements. We are all under considerable pressure, but to leap from a minor disagreement to...to murder?" He scoffed a hollow sound that echoed in the small space. "It's preposterous!"

"Preposterous or not," Max replied evenly, the lines of his jaw set firm, "disagreements don't typically end in one party lying dead. So I must ask, Henry, what, in your mind, would constitute sufficient grounds for such an act?"

Caught off-guard, Henry sputtered, his face reddening. He met Max's gaze, the flickering overhead lamp casting an uneasy glow upon his ruddy complexion. "Now see here, Inspector, you can't possibly think—"

"I don't," Max interrupted, his tone softening just enough to show a hint of his patience for Rosemary—a patience that seemed to extend, albeit strained, towards her family. "But someone has gone to great lengths to ensure Charles will never step foot in America or anywhere else again. And if it wasn't you, we need to find another angle." Max leaned closer, his voice a low rumble of urgency. "We must dig deeper, Henry. What secrets are you not telling me?"

"Secrets do have a way of festering, don't they, Inspector?" Henry sighed loudly, the protective facade of the jolly old elf crumbling to reveal the troubled man beneath. "There's not much to tell," he began hesitantly. "Charles and I had our differences, yes, but nothing that couldn't be settled over a pint or a handshake."

"Yet here we are," Max sighed. "With neither a pint nor a handshake to clear your name."

Rosemary heard Miranda huff and mutter something uncomplimentary under her breath. Her father waved a quelling hand and continued, his voice laced with regret and resignation. "Charles had strong opinions about the R&D department. It was his domain, after all. When it came to Johnathan Palmer, he was adamant—Charles wanted him gone."

Even from the other room, Rosemary could see how his brow creased, and his lips tightened at the memory. "And you disagreed?" Max prodded, his tone understanding but insistent.

"Yes," Henry admitted. "I didn't understand what Charles found so off-putting about the man; frankly, it felt wasteful. Johnathan's work was thorough, and his reports were meticulous. To dismiss such dedication..."

"Yet Charles had the final say," Max noted, leaning back in his chair, the wood creaking softly under his weight.

Henry sighed. "Indeed, he did, as was fair. After all, I didn't have to work with Palmer every day, so I tried to accept that Charles had his reasons. We never spoke of the matter again until last week."

"Go on," Max encouraged, his gaze fixed intently on Henry.

"Another report came through from R&D, below par, just as the ones before it." Henry's voice held a trace of frustration as if he were caught between loyalty and truth. "I couldn't let it pass. I called Charles to my office to discuss the state of affairs."

Max's eyes narrowed slightly, picking up on the tension that threaded through Henry's narrative like a dark undercurrent. "And? What did you say to him?"

"During our discussion, I couldn't help but question the decision once more. Was it entirely necessary to fire Johnathan Palmer?" Henry's query hung in the air.

"Did Charles give you an answer?" Max asked, his voice low.

Henry met Max's gaze squarely.

"Charles... he snapped," Henry muttered, his voice barely rising above a whisper. "He said it was his department, and he'd staff it however he deemed fit."

Max leaned forward, the creaking of his chair breaking the silence that followed. He watched Henry closely, noting how the usually mild-mannered man's jaw clenched at the memory.

"Lois, she was there, you see. Outside the door," Henry confessed, a pang of regret coloring his words. "She must have heard everything. I fear we may have put the poor girl in a difficult position."

"And then?"

"Then," Henry leaned forward in his seat, "Charles did something quite unexpected. His anger abruptly deflated, and he apologized."

Max arched an eyebrow, clearly surprised. "Is that so?"

"Curiously, yes," Henry affirmed. "He conceded that the quality had slipped and admitted he'd been handling the R&D reports himself since Palmer's termination. He agreed to revisit Johnathan's old reports, to learn from them, perhaps improve his own."

"Was there any indication of ill will between you after this?" Max inquired, his question slicing through the tension.

"None whatsoever," Henry responded with a firm shake of his head. "I told him I admired his candor, and we parted amicably with a handshake. Despite our differences, Charles and I always wanted what was best for the company."

"A handshake," Max repeated thoughtfully. "The gesture of gentlemen. Yet here we are, with one gentleman behind bars and another dead. It begs the question, Mr. Woolridge: what did *you* believe was best for the company? Was it Charles at the helm of the American expansion? Or were you jealous that you'd been overlooked for the position?"

Miranda, who had been nearly silent until then, was finally pressed beyond her limit, much to Rosemary's surprise. "My father has answered that question several times already."

"Let the man do his job, Miranda," Henry said, his voice calmer than before. He turned back to Max, his voice resigned. "How could I be overlooked for a position I never put in for? Charles *was* what was best for Woolridge & Sons. Nothing will persuade me to claim otherwise."

Max regarded him with a practiced eye and softened considerably. "Thank you, Henry. I believe you. But we need to find who truly is responsible for Charles's death. Is there anything else you can remember that might be of use? Are you aware of anything that might have put him at odds with someone?" he probed, leaning in slightly.

Henry's gaze wavered, and his fingers found their way into the pocket of the Santa costume to fidget with the fabric. After a moment that stretched too long, he shook his head. "No, Inspector, nothing comes to mind." The words were deliberate and measured, but the hesitation lingered.

"Very well," Max replied, though his tone suggested he believed there was more to be told.

Abruptly, Henry's hand stilled. "There is one thing...the morning he died, Charles mentioned needing to speak with Cecil and me about something urgent."

Max perked. "Did he say what it was regarding, specifically?"

Henry shook his head, sighing heavily. "He didn't. And now..." His voice broke off.

"And now we may never know."

"I believe most of his files and other documents have been sent to Frederick for review, but If it had to do with work, he'd probably have notes in his satchel. Charles tended to write things down."

"His satchel?" Max jotted something in his ever-present notebook. "Nothing like that was found with the body."

Henry shrugged. "I didn't see it in his office when we pulled together his reports. Someone should probably check R&D for it."

"I appreciate your cooperation, Henry. We'll get to the bottom of this," Max reassured him, though the assurance was as much for himself as for the beleaguered man before him.

"Cooperation?" Miranda scoffed. "You practically dragged him here in chains. If you ask me, that behavior doesn't fit the spirit of cooperation."

"Anything you need," Henry said, a tiny spark of gratitude igniting in his weary eyes. "You just ask. I trust you'll do what's right."

Rosemary managed to scramble away from her vantage point near the door and rejoin her parents just as Miranda—who didn't appear to share her father's faith in Max's ability to solve the case—sailed past her family and out the door without saying a word.

THIRTEEN

Rosemary had just enough time to relay what she'd heard to her parents before Max appeared. He cleared his throat, his eyes darting between Cecil and the interrogation room door. "Mr. Woolridge, would you like to speak with your brother now?"

Cecil nodded, his usually jovial face etched with worry lines. "Yes, I believe that would be best. Thank you, Max." He squared his shoulders and strode towards the room, pausing only briefly to squeeze Evelyn's hand before disappearing inside.

Max turned to Rosemary and Evelyn as the door clicked shut, his expression a mixture of apology and resignation. "I'm truly sorry about all this. Henry's a good man, I know, but..." He trailed off, shaking his head. "I'd better get back to work. Make yourselves comfortable."

After depositing a kiss on her cheek, he left. Rosemary watched him go, her mind whirling with the afternoon's events. How had a joyous holiday occasion turned into such a nightmare? She sank back onto the hard wooden bench beside her mother and sighed, wondering with a heavy heart if she wasn't indeed a harbinger of doom. It certainly seemed as though murder followed her everywhere she went.

Evelyn's voice cut through Rosemary's musings. "I do hope Miranda's all right. The poor dear looked so distressed when she left."

"I'm worried about her too. She's so angry, and she had such a determined look in her eye." It was an expression Rosemary recalled well from when they were children, and Miranda had discovered a wrongdoing worth tattling about. Back then, Evelyn's favor alone supplied enough motivation for her to throw the rest of her cousins to the wolves, but Rosemary kept that part to herself.

"As though she had somewhere important to be," Evelyn agreed, absently twisting her pearl necklace. "I hope she's not doing anything rash."

"Oh!" Rosemary's eyes widened suddenly. "What if Miranda's gone to retrieve that satchel Henry mentioned? Think about it. Everyone's still at the office for the charity event. The factory is completely deserted."

Evelyn blinked, considering the possibility. After a short moment, she sprung to her feet and gathered her coat and handbag. "We should follow her. If we hurry, we might just catch her in the act."

Rosemary's jaw dropped as she watched her mother's sudden burst of energy. "Mother, wait. What about Father? We can't just leave him here at the police station!"

Evelyn paused, a small smile playing on her lips. "Oh, Rosemary. When you've been together as long as your father and I, you learn that these things have a certain... flexibility. Especially if you're married to a man as patient as Cecil."

"But—"

"In a long relationship, my dear," Evelyn continued, her voice taking on a sage-like quality, "you're always owing and being owed. It's a delicate balance, you see. Your father will understand."

Rosemary stared, torn between disbelief and a grudging

admiration for her mother's audacity. "I can't believe you're suggesting we just...abandon him here."

"It's not abandonment, dear. It's... a temporary strategic retreat."

"But how will he get back to the office?"

Evelyn finished fastening her coat and turned to face her daughter with a mixture of amusement and mild exasperation. "For heaven's sake. Your father may sometimes be a tad forgetful, but he's far from helpless. Cecil is quite the resourceful fellow when he needs to be." A playful smile danced on her lips as she patted her coat pocket with a conspiratorial wink. "And be thankful he's a tiny bit forgetful. Otherwise, I wouldn't have a key to the factory and office, now would I?"

Rosemary's eyes widened in surprise. "You have a key? But how—"

"No time for questions now, darling," Evelyn interrupted, her voice brimming with enthusiasm. "Come along. We've got a mystery to solve, and time is of the essence!" She strode towards the exit with surprising determination, leaving Rosemary little choice but to hurry after her.

This was not the mother Rosemary knew. Where had this woman with a reckless disregard for the rules come from? Needing to find out, Rosemary quickened her pace to catch up. As she slid into the passenger seat, she couldn't help but wonder what other surprises her mother might have in store for her tonight.

Lady Foxworthy's driver was more than happy to oblige, and she hadn't exaggerated his ability to navigate through the snow-covered streets. Before long, the factory loomed, a hulking silhouette against the night sky. Rosemary's heart raced as she followed her mother through the rear entrance, the key turning in the lock with a soft click.

"Come on, the R&D department is just down this corridor."

"Mother, are you sure about this?" Rosemary hissed, glancing nervously over her shoulder. Her footsteps echoed in the eerie silence, and she was suddenly acutely aware of how close they were to the recent scene of a brutal murder.

Evelyn's response was surprisingly firm, the same thought evidently not having occurred to her. "Quite sure, dear. Now, keep your eyes peeled for anything out of the ordinary."

As they walked through the dye room with vats practically large enough to swim in, Rosemary couldn't shake the feeling of trespassing, but her mother appeared unhampered by the notion. Nevertheless, she kept her voice low as she led Rosemary to the R&D department.

"Start checking those cabinets," Evelyn instructed, rifling through a stack of papers.

Rosemary complied, her hands trembling slightly as she opened drawer after drawer. "Nothing. At least, no satchel full of notes or anything else that looks meaningful to me," she muttered under her breath.

Evelyn's sharp eyes scanned the room, landing briefly on a set of filing drawers, one of which wasn't pushed tightly shut like the others. She moved swiftly, speaking in a measured tone. "Try there next. It looks like someone's been through it recently."

Without warning, a sound pierced the silence—footsteps, growing louder by the second. "Someone's coming."

Evelyn's head snapped up, her eyes wide with alarm. "Quick!" she mouthed, gesturing frantically towards a nearby supply cupboard.

Before Rosemary could fully process what was happening, her mother grabbed her arm and yanked her into the cramped space with surprising speed and agility, pulling the door shut behind them.

Pressed against the back wall of the cupboard, Rosemary stared at her in disbelief. "How did you—" she began, but Evelyn pressed a finger to her lips.

As the footsteps drew nearer, Rosemary marveled at this new side of her mother. The prim and proper Evelyn she knew had vanished, replaced by a woman of action and decisiveness. It was as if years had melted away, revealing hidden depths she had never imagined existed.

Through a narrow crack in the cupboard door, Rosemary watched as a dark figure entered the room. Her heart pounding so loudly she feared it might give away their presence, she wondered fleetingly what had made her think this whole thing was a good idea in the first place.

No matter how understanding her father was, she doubted he would be thrilled if he knew his wife and daughter had broken into his factory and become trapped in a room they weren't meant to be in, a hair's breadth away from the scene of a recent murder, watching someone else who might be the murderer break in as well!

Adrenaline coursed through Rosemary's veins as she reviewed the self-defense lessons she'd recently taken. The perpetrator was slight, not overly muscled, as far as she could tell, but Rosemary remained still as a statue in the hopes they'd get what they wanted and leave before it had to come to violence.

The figure moved with purpose, collecting various items from around the lab, and it felt like an eternity passed before they finally turned around and stepped into a shaft of light. It was Eleanor, and Rosemary felt the tension drain from her body.

"Whatever is she doing?" Evelyn's breath was warm against Rosemary's ear.

She shook her head slightly, eyes fixed on Eleanor. "Gathering samples, it looks like. And some papers."

After what felt like an eternity, she finally left, her footsteps fading down the corridor. Rosemary let out a long, shaky breath.

Evelyn pushed open the cupboard door and stepped out with a grimace. "Well, that was certainly exciting. Although, perhaps we should have confronted her."

Rosemary couldn't help but laugh, the absurdity of the situation hitting her all at once. "Confronted her? Mother, we're the ones skulking about like cat burglars. What would we have said? 'Pardon us, Eleanor, we were just rifling through company property and decided to shimmy into this broom cupboard. Don't mind us!'"

Evelyn's lips twitched. "Well, when you put it that way, I suppose we do look rather suspicious."

Rosemary sighed, her momentary amusement fading as she surveyed the lab one last time, searching for any sign of the elusive satchel. Finding none, she ran a hand through her hair. "This whole expedition was a waste of time. We didn't find Charles's notes or discover anything useful, and Miranda is nowhere to be found."

Evelyn placed a comforting hand on her daughter's shoulder. "Now, now, don't be so hasty. We may not have found what we were looking for, but we did learn something."

"What's that?" Rosemary asked, arching an eyebrow.

"That Eleanor is up to something," Evelyn replied, her voice low and thoughtful. "The question is, what?"

Rosemary pondered this, her mind racing with possibilities. She glanced at her watch, realizing how much time had passed.

"We should head back. Father and Henry will be wondering where we've gone."

FOURTEEN

Rosemary tossed and turned all night, hardly getting a wink of sleep even though Vera and Frederick's luxurious guest bed was so comfortable she was tempted to move in permanently. As the first rays of winter sun began to peek through the drapes, she dressed and readied herself for the day. Dash, however, immune to the lure of a hot cuppa, refused to emerge from beneath the sumptuous eiderdown.

Still bleary-eyed, Rosemary waited in the kitchen until the kettle came to a boil, standing over the fragrant steam. When the leaves had steeped to inky brown perfection, she added a dollop of milk and carried the cup and saucer into the corridor, intending to settle at the dining room table.

Unfortunately, having finally roused, Dash chose that moment to join her, bounding into the hallway and colliding with Rosemary's feet just as she took a sip of her tea. "You furry little menace!" she said with a rueful laugh. "Come on, let's go outside."

Head askance, the dog peered at his owner before promptly taking off down the corridor and disappearing into Frederick's study. Rosemary set her tea on the hall table and hurried after him. Rounding the corner, she opened her mouth to admonish the pup again but closed it with a snap when she noticed her brother hunched over his desk, fast asleep.

A fortress of scattered papers and open ledgers cradling Frederick's head evidenced long hours poring over the R&D

department's files, so dedicated in his quest for answers he'd never even made it to bed. Smiling gently at the sight of him, Rosemary tiptoed inside, not wanting to disturb his rest.

Treading lightly across the room, she scooped Dash into her arms, her gaze lingering on the bookcases filled with leather-bound volumes, their spines aligned with military precision.

Something about the arrangement of the items on the shelves caught her attention—a certain orderliness that was methodical and familiar. Looking around the room, Rosemary noticed that everywhere, the objects had been grouped by category and size, from a collection of antique inkwells to a series of globes charting the world's changing borders.

A row of framed photographs, perched at eye level along the mantle, had been angled just so, ensuring that the faces within could be seen without the glare of the morning light. Rosemary peered around again, a slow smile spreading across her face.

Lost in her observation, she almost didn't notice Frederick stirring, the movement subtle as he shifted beneath the weight of his exhaustion. His eyelids fluttered open to reveal eyes red-rimmed and bleary from a night devoid of sleep.

An involuntary groan escaped his lips as he attempted to straighten up, his body protesting the awkward angle at which he had slumbered against the unforgiving wooden desk. Squinting into the soft morning light spilling into the study, he caught sight of his sister just as her gaze returned to him with an enigmatic smile.

"Rosemary?" he croaked, "What has you looking so annoyingly cheerful this early in the day?"

"Oh, nothing of great consequence." She tucked a loose strand of hair behind her ear as Dash jumped out of her arms and into Frederick's lap. "I've simply unraveled a tiny mystery, dear brother. I believe I know your secret."

Frederick arched an eyebrow, a lazy half-smile replacing his look of bewilderment as he petted the dog's furry head. "And what secret might that be? That I'm hopelessly devoted to my work or that I have an affinity for falling asleep in the most uncomfortable of positions?"

"You know good and well what I'm talking about," Rosemary chuckled softly, nodding towards the mantle, "though I don't suppose Vera's figured it out yet. What would she say if she knew you and her precious *Wads* were in cahoots?"

"She won't say anything as long as you keep it to yourself, *dear sister*," Frederick replied pointedly. "An organized home makes Vera happy. How it becomes organized shouldn't be of any consequence."

"The means justify the ends, as it were? In this case, you might not be entirely incorrect. When did you get to be so wise, anyway?"

Frederick smiled devilishly and wiggled his eyebrows. "If you remember, Vera isn't the first dame to have made my acquaintance."

"You and Dash have more in common than I thought." Rosemary couldn't help but chuckle.

"Never mind that now," Frederick said, brow creasing, suddenly all business as he rifled through the files and pulled out a particular document. "Take a look at this. I think I know why something about Drakeford's paperwork didn't sit right with me. Look at the handwriting—doesn't it match this sample?"

He handed her another paper, his gaze intense and searching. Rosemary studied the script closely, comparing the loops and strokes of ink that were unmistakably similar. She nodded slowly, her earlier mirth replaced by a newfound gravity. "It's a match, Frederick. But what does it mean? Whose handwriting is it?"

"That's the odd thing. It's Johnathan Palmer's." Frederick let the revelation hang in the air for a long moment, during which Vera entered the study looking well-rested and fresh as a daisy.

Noting Frederick's disheveled appearance, she hurried over to his side. "You look dreadful, darling. Did you sleep in here?" Her keen eyes shifted from Rosemary, holding the incriminating document, to Frederick with his sleeves rolled up and his eyes bright, both caught in the act of discovery. "What is it? What did you find?"

"We aren't certain, precisely," Rosemary answered, "but there seems to be a connection between Sam Drakeford and Johnathan Palmer. I think we'd better rouse Father."

"I think you're right." Vera bustled back out, returning soon after with both Cecil and Evelyn in tow.

Cecil examined the documents, his expression etched with the weariness of one who had navigated his fair share of crises. "I've had enough of this nonsense," he spat. "Cryptic findings and secret allegiances. Not at my company. Not now, not ever."

Without hesitation, he strode around to the other side of Frederick's desk and picked up the telephone. After a moment, he spoke into the mouthpiece with a clipped, "Drakeford? It's Cecil Woolridge. Not well, under the circumstances. We need to speak. Immediately. I'm afraid I must insist. Yes, I'm aware of the weather, but I'm afraid I must insist. All right then. We'll await your arrival."

"We could have gone to him," Frederick said when his father disconnected the line.

Cecil shook his head. "It's unwise to beard a lion in his own den."

"Fair point. On a related note, perhaps it's best if Father and I speak to Sam in private. How would it look to have wives and sisters present during the discussion of a delicate business matter?"

Whatever sharp retort Vera might have answered with was cut off when Evelyn jabbed an elbow into her ribs.

"That's just fine, dear. When he arrives, why don't you entertain Mr. Drakeford in here? You want to set the right mood for a difficult conversation. The study is a serious room for a serious matter."

"Quite right," Cecil agreed and said to Frederick. "Quite right. Your mother has a keen sense for these things. The study it is."

Vera looked like she'd swallowed a piece of rotten fish, but later, when the doorbell rang, she allowed herself to be led upstairs without protest. Rosemary followed. But when Vera would have turned right to enter her private sitting room, Evelyn dragged her to the left and into one of the guest bedrooms. Again, Rosemary followed.

"What are you doing?"

"You think I haven't learned a thing or two from my nosy children?" Evelyn—the Woolridge family's dignified matriarch —dropped her hands and knees beside the heating grate and motioned the others to join her.

"We always seem to be skulking around and listening at doors," Vera grumbled. "Solving mysteries while the men bluster and bluff."

"That's just how it is for women, dear. Most simply learn to live with their lot in life. The clever ones, like us, find ways to get around it," Evelyn said, surprising her daughter, who never thought she would hear such a thing come out of her mother's mouth.

Eyes shining with determination, she held a finger over her lips and carefully opened the grate.

The men's voices rose up clearly through the hole in the floor while the women enjoyed their birds-eye view through the holes in the grate and listened to every word.

"Nice place you've got here, Mr. Woolridge," Drakeford said, keeping his tone pleasant and light. "What was so important it couldn't wait until later?"

"Mr. Drakeford," Cecil began, his voice steady and unwavering, betraying none of the frustration simmering beneath his composure. "It has come to our attention that you've had dealings with Johnathan Palmer. In light of the situation, I must ask: what, precisely, is the nature of your connection?"

"Johnathan Palmer?" Drakeford echoed with a practiced nonchalance contradicted by the steady tapping of his fingers against the arm of the chair. "You don't mean that chap you lot mentioned having sacked, do you?"

A silent battle of wills played out between them, the air growing thick enough for Rosemary to feel it through the floorboards. Her father's gaze never wavered; clearly, he wouldn't be so easily appeased by deflection or deceit.

Frederick passed over the incriminating documents. "We've seen Palmer's hand before," he said smoothly, holding Drakeford's gaze with unnerving calmness. "Your denial lacks substance when his signature is on documents from your company's archives."

Drakeford paused, the rhythm of his drumming fingers stilling. A shadow passed over his face briefly before resignation settled there. He exhaled slowly, withdrawing into himself for a moment before speaking.

"Very well," he conceded, his early confidence draining. "I wasn't aware of the connection until the unfortunate incident involving your brother's arrest."

Cecil leaned back in his chair, the leather creaking softly beneath him. His eyes, sharp as flint, remained fixed on Drakeford, searching for any hint of duplicity. "Samuel," he said, the use of the man's first name punctuating the gravity of his disappointment, "your father built his legacy on integrity. Had you been forthright upon hearing of Palmer's involvement, we might have averted this entire debacle."

He let the words hang in the air, heavy with implication. Drakeford's lips parted, a half-formed apology hovering in the charged silence between them. His hand, resting on the mahogany table, twitched slightly, betraying his attempt at composure.

"Please, understand," he began, his voice tinged with desperation, "my intentions were never to—"

Cecil raised a hand, silencing Drakeford mid-sentence. The air grew still, and even the grandfather clock in the corner seemed to withhold its ticking.

"Unfortunately," Cecil said, his tone firm yet not unkind, "your actions—or rather, your inactions—have consequences." He paused, allowing the gravity of his words to sink in. "We've invested much in you, not merely in terms of finance but also trust and reputation. However, in light of your behavior, we must reassess our involvement with your company."

The muscles in Drakeford's jaw tightened, and his eyes clouded over, the gleam of ambition that usually inhabited them dulled by the sting of reproach.

"Of course," he replied, his voice steady despite the clear upset. "I understand your position." He stood, straightening the cuffs of his tailored suit and extending a hand towards Cecil to show respect. Your family has been more than fair. If this is your decision, I will accept it with the dignity that the situation warrants."

Frederick nodded. "Appreciate your understanding."

Having retrieved his coat, Drakeford made one final comment that was brushed aside. "I do hope you'll change your mind."

"That wasn't the reaction I was expecting," Rosemary whispered, then went quiet when Frederick's voice carried up through the vent.

"I say. He seemed a good egg about it all. Are you certain we haven't made a hasty decision? It's not too late to reconsider."

"It's well past time for that," Cecil assured his son. "A man willing to deceive with small lies will not draw the line at telling large ones. I can't trust him. This encounter has left a bad taste in my mouth. It would take quite a lot to convince me to deal with Sam Drakeford again."

Kicking his feet out in front of him, Frederick steepled his fingers before saying to his father. "I'm surprised, honestly. I'd have expected you to have more sympathy. Isn't it you who always taught us that everyone deserves a second chance?"

"Quite right." Cecil nodded. "I do believe in second chances. I have, however, found their application to be more fruitful in matters of a personal nature and far less in business. Hurt feelings may be difficult to mend, but they're less expensive than throwing in our lot with the wrong sorts of people."

"Speaking of the wrong sorts, you ladies might as well come back downstairs." Frederick tilted back his head and smirked up at the grate. "I'm sure you've heard everything that happened, so there will be no need to repeat the course of events."

FIFTEEN

Too late to join them for dinner, Max arrived looking ever more worse for wear than he had the previous day at the station. Having been apprised of Frederick's find, he strode into the study on a gust of wind, his hat dusted with the snow that whipped to and fro outside the windows.

"Max, you look a fright," Rosemary said as he leaned down to kiss her cheek. "Come in and warm yourself at the fire. Vera and Freddie are out back, braving the garden with Dash. Stella can fetch them if you like." Taking his arm, she guided him closer to the fireplace.

Stella made to rise from her position between Evelyn and Cecil on the sofa, but Max held up a hand.

"Don't trouble yourself. I wish I could stay, but I'm afraid I haven't much time." His voice resonated with urgency. "Nor do I have particularly cheerful news. The hunt for Johnathan Palmer is at something of a standstill. It seems he's moved since leaving Woolridge & Sons, and we've no forwarding address. Now that we know about the Drakeford connection, there's another angle to explore, but it's slow going, given the holiday and this infernal storm. Rest assured, every possible lead is being pursued. I'm seeing to it."

"Your dedication is not lost on us, Max." Cecil clapped a hand on Max's shoulder. "I understand there are procedures you must follow, and I trust your judgment."

Rosemary felt a rush of gratitude and admiration for her father's ability to remain objective even in trying circumstances. Max breathed out with relief, the lines around his eyes becoming slightly less pronounced as the frown he'd been wearing smoothed away.

Uncle Henry was no murderer. Rosemary would bet her best paintbrush on that. Someone else must have killed Charles, but Max had to arrest the most viable suspect, and that suspect was Uncle Henry. She'd have done the same in his shoes.

"I'd give anything to let Henry out right now," he admitted, "but I'm bound by the law. It's a frustrating position to have found myself in—again."

Evelyn stepped forward, her grace undiminished by the circumstances, her hand finding Cecil's. "We all know Henry is innocent," she said with a calm certainty that settled like a blanket over the room. "In time, the truth will prevail."

Speechless, Rosemary simply stared. She'd grown so accustomed to steeling herself against Evelyn's sharp tongue that she found this softer side of her mother almost unnerving.

"Thank you, Evelyn," Max said in a voice that sounded as though he felt the same way. "Truly, your support means a great deal. I must be going now, but I'll be in touch. Take care of yourself, Rosemary." He bade them all goodbye, tipping his hat before departing again into the bitter chill.

When he'd gone, Cecil sighed wearily and quietly excused himself, leaving Rosemary alone with her mother and sister.

Evelyn's gaze lingered pensively on the frost-laced windowpanes for a long moment. "It is dreadfully near Christmas," she murmured, her voice laced with both concern and bitterness. "And Miranda...that poor dear must be beside herself with the notion of her father incarcerated during the holiday season."

Rosemary swallowed back the automatic response, remembering instead the genuine distress that had clouded Miranda's eyes when speaking of her father. Compassion tempered her impulse. If her mother could change her spots, Rosemary decided, so could she.

"Still," Evelyn continued, her voice closer to its usual sharp tone. "One might assume that having a daughter courting the chief inspector would safeguard one's family from repeated arrests. Clearly, one would be mistaken."

All of Rosemary's warm and fuzzy feelings evaporated under the heat of renewed annoyance.

Turning to face Evelyn square-on, her words were measured but firm. "Max has already risked more than enough for our family," she said, an edge of steel in her voice that had seldom been heard before. "I won't be the one to ask him for favors, not when it could cost him everything he's worked for. That might be your way of working around things, but it won't be mine."

Evelyn looked as though she'd been slapped, and while Rosemary felt justified in her words, she immediately regretted the sting they'd caused. Still too angry to apologize, she spun on her heel and stalked out of the study.

Rosemary found herself drifting towards the sitting room where she discovered her father, busy resurrecting remnants of Christmases past. She paused at the threshold, observing him hunched over the miniature train set with a craftsman's precision. Cecil's hands, steady and sure, wielded a magnifying glass and paintbrush as though they were instruments of delicate surgery, breathing life back into the chipped and broken toys.

Sensing he wasn't alone, he looked up from his task, his eyes crinkling warmly at the sight of his daughter.

"Ah, Rosemary, come sit." With the hand holding the glass, he gestured to the tiny, fractured world sprawled out before him. "Just giving these old companions some much-needed attention. Your brother would have hated to see them in disrepair."

He handed her a figurine whose paint had worn nearly off, making its identification almost impossible. "Is this a dog or a cat?" Rosemary asked.

"It can be whatever you'd like it to be," her father said with a wink, "though I believe it's a puppy. If I recall correctly, his name was Spot."

The memory came rushing back. "Yes, he was Lionel's favorite," Rosemary murmured, allowing herself a moment to reminisce about the brother whose absence had left a void no amount of time could fill. She watched as her father returned to his meticulous work, each stroke of his brush another memory preserved.

In the quiet company of her father, the careful restoration of Lionel's cherished train set offered Rosemary a moment of reprieve as the weight of suspicion and danger lifted ever so slightly from her shoulders.

After a few moments, Rosemary looked up at her father with newfound admiration. "This is much more difficult than I imagined," she admitted, her eyes strained from squinting.

"But you're an artist, dear."

"I paint land and seascapes, not intricate little figurines." After several moments of easy silence, she added, "I've not the faintest idea how you can maintain such patience."

Cecil paused, setting down the glass to peer at Rosemary with a thoughtful expression. "And I, my dear, often ponder over your resilience and fortitude. To do what you do, to uncover the hidden truths and face danger head-on, requires a mettle, I daresay, which is much rarer than patience."

"I'm not talking of the trains. I meant Mother," she huffed, her voice tinged with exasperation, "how have you managed all these years? She can be...decidedly exacting."

Cecil paused, contemplating the locomotive before him, his hands steady even as the question hung in the air like a delicate cloud of steam. He looked up at Rosemary, his eyes reflecting a lifetime of quiet understanding.

"Your mother has always had strong convictions, dear," he said softly, a small smile playing at the corners of his lips. "But it was that very fire that drew me to her. Evelyn captivated me from the moment we met." His gaze became distant for a heartbeat, lost in a memory only he could see.

"Despite appearances, her worries concerning Andrew, and now Max were never rooted in social standing or wealth. Your grandmother was adamant Evelyn should marry a man of substantial means. But Evelyn defied her and chose me instead." He glanced up, locking eyes with Rosemary, ensuring she grasped the gravity of his next words. "Evelyn's fear has always been loss. After Lionel..." His voice trailed off.

The tension in Rosemary's shoulders tightened, an invisible coil wound to its breaking point. "I'm aware of how much she's endured, Father. But so have I. Grief is a familiar companion to us both."

"Your heart has been tried by fire, my dear," Cecil said, his voice a soothing balm to her chafing spirit. "But remember, your mother bears scars too, ones that time has yet to heal fully. She only seeks to protect you from further harm."

"Protect or suffocate, sometimes the line is dreadfully thin," Rosemary murmured, her attention returning to the train set.

"Thin it may be," Cecil acknowledged, cleaning his paintbrush, "but love seldom measures its strength. It acts, often imperfectly, but always fervently."

"One thing I've learned through all this—through the cases,

through life—is that you can't prevent loss. Andrew's passing wasn't crime or villainy that took him from me; it was his heart." Rosemary's words hung heavy in the air.

"Indeed." Cecil met her eyes with a look of gentle reproof. "And while we navigate these turbulent waters, we must be mindful not to anchor ourselves to resentment."

Cecil reached out, placing a comforting hand atop hers—a silent acknowledgment of shared sorrow. Rosemary's eyes softened, the harsh edges of her frustration blurring into something more akin to understanding.

"We can never judge another's pain, can we?" Cecil broke the stillness with a gentle voice, not looking up from his task. The magnifying glass clutched in his other hand amplified the seriousness in his eyes. "We can judge their actions, though, and your mother's have always shown, no matter what else, that she cares about her children and would do anything for you."

"That's not something all children can say about their parents." Cecil paused, setting the brush down and gazing at his daughter pointedly.

A log shifted in the fireplace, sending a flurry of sparks up the chimney. Rosemary's expression wavered, caught between the fierce independence that drove her and the longing for maternal approval that lingered beneath the surface.

"Evelyn will come round in her own time; you've got to let her get there on her own. Like someone else I know," Cecil added, the hint of a smile playing at the corner of his mouth as he bestowed upon her a conspiratorial wink.

"Thank you, Father," Rosemary whispered, allowing herself the luxury of leaning into his steady presence. "Your patience, it seems, extends to understanding Mother in ways I am still learning."

Cecil nodded, his attention returning to the miniature train car in his hands. "We all have our roles to play, Rosemary. Some mend trains. Others mend hearts. And some," he added, a hint of pride in his voice, "uncover truths that would otherwise remain shrouded in darkness."

"I'm sorry about Uncle Henry."

"You've nothing to be sorry for," Cecil replied, the corners of his lips twitching upward in an attempt at reassurance. "This is but a dreadful misunderstanding. Henry hasn't a sinister bone in his body. Truth has a way of revealing itself, especially when it's most obscured by doubt."

Rosemary nodded, finding solace in her father's steadfast belief. Yet she couldn't help but feel the weight of unease that lingered like a persistent fog in the air, seeping into every corner of the room.

She also felt the weight of remorse for the way she'd thought about her mother, but when Rosemary went looking, she discovered Evelyn had already retired to the guest bedroom.

Sixteen

"We're meant to spend Christmas Eve ice skating on the pond and taking carriage rides through the village," Stella lamented the following day after receiving word that Leonard and the children had yet to board the train out of Oxford and were unlikely to arrive in time to open their Christmas stockings.

Stella paced the sitting room like a caged lioness while outside, the snow continued to fall in thick curtains, coating the paths that should have been filled with her approaching family in a thick layer of fluffy white snow.

Ever the optimist, Vera had corralled everyone before the tree as if she hoped festive garlands and twinkling lights could somehow lighten their spirits. She'd planned for the perfect Christmas, and when reality fell short, resolved to salvage what joy she could. And yet, her smile never quite reached her eyes as she moved about the towering evergreen with a grace born of sheer willpower. Rosemary watched as her hands tenderly smoothed a ribbon here and adjusted an ornament there.

"Treading a hole in the carpet won't make the snow stop falling, you know," Frederick snapped from where he sat at the table next to his father, poring over still more ledgers and files.

"Pardon me if the novelty of a murder investigation has begun to wear off," Stella retorted, her voice rising to a fever pitch.

"At least you're not in jail like Uncle Henry. Things could be worse."

"Darling," Vera softly admonished Frederick, who finally glanced up from the document he scrutinized to meet his wife's disapproving gaze. "It's Lyn's first Christmas, after all, and Stella is simply afraid she will miss the whole thing."

With some chagrin, Frederick smiled apologetically. "Perhaps we ought to light the Yule log now, then?" he suggested. "It might lift everyone's spirits." He nodded towards his mother, who sat rigid on the chaise longue, her gaze locked onto the dancing flames of the fireplace.

Rosemary's heart ached for them all, especially Henry, who would spend Christmas Eve behind bars instead of with his loved ones unless a miracle occurred before nightfall. The shrill ring of the telephone cut through the muffled despair, and Cecil looked up from his stack of papers, startled.

"Get that for me, will you, Rosie?" Vera called from the stepladder, where she perched, fussing with the star at the top of the tree.

"Woolridge residence, Rosemary speaking," she spoke into the telephone with a practiced cheerfulness that fell flat under the circumstances.

"Ah, Rosemary, my dear!" The unmistakable cadence of Lady Foxworthy's voice crackled over the line, bright and unfettered by the gloom that had settled in the Woolridge home. "I do hope I'm not catching you at an inconvenient time?"

"Of course not, Beatrice," Rosemary replied, a genuine smile creeping across her lips for the first time that day. "How may we assist you?"

"Assist me?" Lady Foxworthy chuckled, a sound as clear as church bells. "No, no, my dear, it is I who wish to offer a bit of excitement! How does tea at the Grand Lion sound? We've booked the best table in the dining room and wish to share some news that I daresay will bring a welcome bit of holiday cheer to your household!"

"That sounds wonderful, but I'm afraid we're quite snowed in at the moment."

"Oh, don't you worry about that. I've called Blacks. They're sending a carriage round for you, and we won't take no for an answer. And do tell everyone to dress warmly. The weather outside is frightful, but the fires at the Grand Lion are delightful, rest assured. Four o'clock sharp!"

Lady Foxworthy rattled off some instructions and disconnected the line before Rosemary could protest again. She turned back to the room and repeated the conversation. "Everyone, Beatrice has extended an invitation for tea at the Grand Lion. She has some news she believes will lift our spirits. Or rather she and someone else, because she used the word 'we' during the invitation."

For a moment, there was a collective pause, the prospect of good news—any good news— beginning to thaw the icy veneer of the room. Frederick closed the file in front of him, and even Stella ceased her pacing, the ghost of curiosity flickering in her eyes.

"News?" echoed Evelyn, her frosty demeanor giving way to intrigue. "What sort of news?"

"I bet it's an engagement," Stella mused. "Between her and Mr. Abernathy."

"Engagement?" Evelyn scoffed, the word crystallizing like breath on cold air. She eyed Stella with a coolness that rivaled the weather. "They've known each other for all of two days."

"Sometimes, Mother, that's all it takes." The cheeky retort popped out of Stella's mouth before she had time to think her words through.

Disapproval evident in the slight downturn of her lips, Evelyn replied, "There's no need to be crude, dear."

But Stella had already dismissed her mother's skepticism with a practiced ease borne of many such exchanges. "You've got to hand it to her. She doesn't waste any time, does she?"

"I haven't told you the best part," Rosemary continued, warmth returning to her cheeks. "She's sending round a horse-drawn carriage to fetch us, so it seems Christmas hasn't entirely given up on us yet."

Frederick let out a low whistle when he stepped into the Grand Lion Hotel's opulent dining room. "Bloody hell."

"I'll say," Vera agreed, leaning towards Rosemary and Stella conspiratorially when she saw Lady Foxworthy's companion. "It seems Mr. Abernathy is a rare breed of man more likely to undersell than embellish. It does beg the question—again—as to where his money comes from, doesn't it? Presuming he's footing the bill."

"Trust me, Beatrice can settle her own account."

Decorated to the hilt in shades of silver and gold and lit with the glow of a half dozen opulent chandeliers, the dining room veritably sparkled with holiday cheer. Several large windows looked out onto the glittering streets of London, leaving Rosemary with the impression that she was standing inside an enormous snow globe.

The clinking of fine crystal and the soft laughter of well-lubricated patrons created a pleasantly festive atmosphere. Seated at the head of one table, Mr. Abernathy wore an expression of utter beguilement, his gaze fixed to his right on Lady

Foxworthy, resplendent in a gown of emerald silk that coordinated perfectly with the decor.

Her silver hair swept into a soft, intricate chignon, gleamed under the light like polished frost. One hand gesticulated animatedly with a long-stemmed wine glass; the other remained close to Mr. Abernathy's arm, reaching over every so often to gently caress it.

Rosemary was almost grateful poor Uncle Henry wasn't around to witness the blatant display of affection. From the looks of it, any chance he'd had with Beatrice had disappeared under a cloud of Mr. Abernathy's expensive cologne.

"Evelyn, darling, there you are. Cecil, everyone. Welcome to our little celebration." Lady Foxworthy beamed almost as brightly as the tapered candlesticks.

Rosemary felt a twinge of guilt for shaming her mother out of the full Grand Lion guest experience. However, it evaporated almost immediately when Evelyn caught sight of Miranda and veritably shoved Stella out of the way in her haste to mend fences.

"You poor thing," Evelyn fussed over her niece with an easy affection that threatened to further deflate Stella's tentatively buoyant mood. Miranda's answering smile was more polite than the one she directed towards the rest of the family, but for once, she appeared less than eager to bask in the glow of her favorite aunt's attention.

"We're most delighted that you could join us, particularly given the unusual circumstances that have befallen us this holiday," Mr. Abernathy added, quite sincerely as far as Rosemary could tell. When everyone had tucked in, he cleared his throat loudly, commanding the table's attention. "Before we get started, Beatrice and I have some exciting news to share."

The crystal clinked softly as Lady Foxworthy raised her

glass, her expression suddenly solemn amid the celebratory mood. "It's a small consolation, of course, but we're hoping to to shine a bright spot into the darkness, if you will."

Miranda's eyes narrowed warily, but Lady Foxworthy's continued to shine. "Thomas and I have found ourselves in something of a fortunate position," she continued, her hand again finding his on the table.

"Indeed," Mr. Abernathy chimed in, his voice steady and sure. "And we agree that we'd be utter fools to walk away from a golden opportunity—particularly one that's fallen so neatly into our laps." The pair exchanged a loaded glance.

Stella elbowed Rosemary underneath the table. "What did I tell you?" she whispered out of the corner of her mouth.

But her smugness came a moment too soon when Mr. Abernathy's next statement seemed to veer off the expected course. "We believe in both the legacy and future of Woolridge & Sons, and with Sam Drakeford out of the picture, it was an easy decision for us both—"

"—To commit to investing in the company," Lady Foxworthy finished for him.

A collective sigh of relief mingled with surprise escaped from the family, the expectation of wedding bells dissolving into the reality of business salvation.

"I must confess, I've never been one to trust easily," said Mr. Abernathy, "and Sam Drakeford—well, something about him has always struck me as...off. He may shop at the same establishments as the rest of us, dress in finery, and speak with a silver tongue, but beneath that veneer, he's nothing more than a common fraud."

His words hung heavy in the air, leaving an acrid taste that not even the sumptuous wine could wash away. The family exchanged uneasy glances, the jovial energy seeping out like air from a punctured balloon.

Looking upon her dearest friends and their less-than-enthused faces, Lady Foxworthy appeared pained. She had hoped for cheers, smiles, and some semblance of relief to lift the melancholy spirits that had taken hold of the Woolridge family but instead was met with a silence that bore the weight of a thousand unspoken worries.

"Surely this news should lighten your hearts," she implored, her voice laced with a gentle reproach. "It's Christmas Eve, after all!"

Miranda, who had been silent throughout the exchange, finally spoke up, her voice cutting through the tension with a sharpness that laid bare her inner turmoil. "With all due respect, Lady Foxworthy, it's hard to find joy when my father languishes behind bars on false accusations." Her eyes, fiery with indignation, locked onto Rosemary's, sending an unspoken challenge across the table.

"Only a fool would believe that Henry Woolridge—a man of such kindness and integrity—could be capable of something as vile as murder," Lady Foxworthy declared, her conviction resonating in the hush that followed.

"Yes," Miranda agreed, her gaze still fixed on Rosemary, who shifted uncomfortably under the scrutiny. "Only a fool."

The words lingered between them for a long moment before the clinking of glasses and the low hum of other diners provided a welcome reprieve for Vera to excuse herself to the loo. "I'll join you," Stella said quickly, beating a hasty retreat from the awkward moment while Evelyn merely turned her attention to the men's conversation as if nothing unusual had transpired.

"I think I need a refill," Rosemary said, rising also. She

moved towards the bar, her need for a respite from the unyielding tension guiding each step. The warmth of the Grand Lion's festive decor contrasted sharply with the frigid atmosphere she'd left behind.

"Whisky, neat," she told the barman, leaning against the polished mahogany. She welcomed the fiery burn, hoping it might thaw the chill that had settled into her bones.

As the amber liquid swirled in her glass, a commotion stirred in Rosemary's peripheral vision—a sudden movement, a gasp. She turned just in time to see Miranda stand abruptly, her chair scraping back with an urgency that sent whispers rippling through the room. Her cousin's face was devoid of color, her usual fiery composure replaced by a haunting pallor.

"Miranda, my dear, whatever is the matter?" Lady Foxworthy's voice, frothing with concern, rose above the gentle clatter of the dining room.

Already hastening away from the table, Miranda didn't stop. A few other diners paused, mid-conversation, forks suspended in the air, for a long moment, watching the spectacle unfold.

"Miranda!" she called again, her call trailing into the din as Miranda vanished.

Rosemary set her glass down with more force than intended, the whisky sloshing dangerously close to the rim. "What happened? Where did she go?"

Bewildered, Lady Foxworthy shook her head. "I haven't the foggiest idea. We were chatting, and then, out of nowhere, she turned white as a sheet and fled." Her eyes searched the space where Miranda had been as if the answers might be found in the lingering silence.

"Did she say anything before she left?"

"Nothing at all. We were discussing the American expansion one moment, and the next—she was gone."

Rosemary's mind whirred with possibilities, each more troubling than the last. What could have prompted such a dramatic exit? She rounded on Lady Foxworthy with a furrowed brow and asked, her voice low and insistent, "Miranda wouldn't dash off over business talk. What exactly did you say to her?"

"I merely mentioned the American expansion."

"There must have been something—a trigger. Be specific, Beatrice," Evelyn implored.

"Well, I was expressing my gratitude, really. If it weren't for that new secretary, Lois, and her...let's call it *lack of aptitude*, Thomas and I might never have crossed paths." Her eyes held a distant gleam, her thoughts clearly drifting to the man who had captured her affections so swiftly.

Rosemary's gaze narrowed, a predator focused on its prey, as she leaned closer. "How did that happen, exactly?"

The question pulled Lady Foxworthy from her reverie. "Oh, well," she replied with a dismissive wave of her hand, "Lois called me, said there was some urgency or another, and asked if I would mind terribly dropping off my check for the charity event in person."

"Interesting," Rosemary mused, storing away every detail as the clinking of glasses and hum of conversation around her faded into the background. The pieces were beginning to form a picture, but the edges were still blurred.

Returning from the loo several steps ahead of Vera, Stella overheard the comment. "Interesting and odd," she said, her voice sharper than the cutlery. "Considering how many donations arrived through the post. I saw a whole stack of them on Lois's desk."

Lady Foxworthy's eyebrows rose towards her hairline. "Precisely my thought. I've never been asked to deliver my donation to the office, but the poor girl sounded so beleaguered I thought it best to follow her instructions."

"What else do you suppose has slipped through the cracks under Lois's watch?" Evelyn said.

"Never mind that for now," Rosemary pressed, her voice low and insistent. "What else did you say to Miranda?"

Leaning back, Lady Foxworthy thought for a moment. "Well, I happened to mention that I'd overheard Charles speaking with Henry," Rosemary noted the faint crease of confusion between her brows. "They were discussing Eleanor taking up a job in America."

"Go on." Rosemary's intuition prickled.

Her voice dipped to a conspiratorial whisper. "I simply suggested that perhaps it was Eleanor who had captured Charles's heart." Her eyes held a glint of mischief, unaware of the gravity her words carried.

Evelyn gripped Rosemary's arm, her eyes following Miranda's path across the dining room. "It's clear as day, isn't it?" she whispered, her voice dripping with self-satisfaction. "The poor girl was in love with Charles, and he chose Eleanor instead."

"Surely you're not implying that girl had anything to do with Charles's murder?" Lady Foxworthy demanded.

"Of course not, Beatrice," Evelyn reassured, "I'm merely concerned for my niece. She's been through enough, hasn't she?"

A flicker of a theory ignited behind Rosemary's thoughtful stare, but she didn't dare speak it out loud. If Miranda had harbored affections for Charles, perhaps she'd seen herself emigrating to America alongside him—maybe even as his wife.

A whole new life dangled and then whisked from within her reach like a cruel joke. Remembering how she'd felt when she lost Andrew, Rosemary couldn't imagine learning such a secret so soon after his death. It would have thrown her into an emotional tailspin.

"Excuse us, Beatrice. I need to have a word with my mother." Rosemary pulled Evelyn from her seat and around the corner into the vestibule, where they'd checked their coats on the way in. She answered Vera's questioning glance with a shake of her head and kept a firm grip on her mother's arm. When they were out of Lady Foxworthy's earshot, she declared, "We ought to follow her."

"Miranda? You recall how splendidly that went last time," her mother reminded her dryly.

"Think about it: if she was in love with Charles and thought Eleanor won his affections, it could be catastrophic for her state of mind."

Evelyn cast a wary glance into the street, where snowflakes danced like tiny specters beneath the lamplight. "We're in the middle of a snowstorm."

Rosemary craned her neck to peer out the window and up at the darkening sky. "It looks like we're nearing the end of it. The roads are empty, and it isn't as though we're without transportation." She tipped her head towards Black's line of horse-drawn carriages waiting outside the hotel. "And besides, we aren't far from the office. Eleanor has been working there all week. That's probably where Miranda is headed."

"All right," her mother agreed, though she still appeared doubtful.

Frederick poked his head around the corner, his face alight with curiosity when he saw his mother donning her coat. "Where are you off to in such a hurry?"

"To find Miranda. She's heartbroken, and comforting her is the least we can do under the circumstances," Evelyn said, suddenly on board with Rosemary's suggestion.

"Perhaps you shouldn't go alone," he suggested, his face etched with concern. "Shall I accompany you?"

"This requires a delicate sensibility, Freddie," Rosemary insisted. "Trust me, you'd be well advised to refrain from inserting yourself into the equation. Former Lothario or not, the soft underbelly of feminine intrigue is not your battlefield."

Evelyn turned to her son with a soft yet resolute smile. "She's right, dear. If Miranda is heartbroken over a man, no man is safe."

Frederick appeared poised to argue but, smartly recognizing that he was indeed well out of his depth, held his hands up in surrender.

"Go back and tell your father where we've gone. We'll be as quick as we can," Evelyn ordered her son.

"Where are you going?" Unable to bear being left behind, Stella followed her brother from the table and arrived just in time to follow her mother and sister out the door.

"To find Miranda. You're going back to Frederick and Vera's with your father, young lady," Evelyn instructed briskly, attempting to shepherd her daughter back into the fold of safety. But Stella bristled, her arms crossing defiantly over her chest.

"Look here, Mother," Stella retorted sharply, the heat of her words belying the cold air that nipped at their cheeks. "I may be your youngest daughter, but I am not a young lady! I have children of my own. I'm every bit the adult that Rosemary is." She might as well have stomped her feet for all it did to improve her position—or soften Evelyn's resolve.

"Stella." Despite the warning in Evelyn's tone, Stella remained unmoved.

"I'll do what I please," she stated flatly. It was evident at that moment that the coddling threads of motherhood would no longer bind her willful spirit.

With a sigh of exasperation, Evelyn conceded the battle. "Very well. Go get your coat."

As soon as the door closed behind Stella, Evelyn said, "Come along now before she comes back." Instead of heading for the carriage, she grabbed Rosemary's arm and pulled her towards where Lady Abernathy's town car and driver waited.

"Did you see my niece leave?" Evelyn demanded as she practically shoved Rosemary inside, followed, and slammed the door behind her.

"I did, mum."

"Follow her, please."

"As you wish." Jensen pulled out just as Stella stepped onto the sidewalk, her face a mask of fury as she watched the car drive off into the darkening night without her. Rosemary caught her eye through the icy car window and mouthed an apology.

"You do realize, don't you," Rosemary informed her mother, "that this could be construed as theft?"

Evelyn declined to answer.

SEVENTEEN

His face impassive, Jensen followed Miranda's black sedan through the nearly deserted streets of London, keeping far enough back not to be noticed by his quarry. The car's tire tracks provided a convenient trail until the storm picked up, and the spitting snow began to fall in thick flakes, quickly covering the street in a white blanket. Evelyn's lips curled into a satisfied grin - her prediction about the weather had come true.

When they reached the Woolridge & Sons office building, Jensen parked around the side, out of sight, and promised to wait there until Rosemary and Evelyn emerged.

"We might need to offer him a generous Christmas tip," Rosemary said as they darted across the street, ducking behind parked cars, the snow helpfully muffling their footsteps. "Or give him a job when he gets fired for leaving his employer in the lurch."

Inside, the space that had felt airy in the light of day stretched out before them, bathed in shadows. Gone was the bustling energy and the symphony of telephone bells and typewriter keys, replaced by an eerie stillness that made the hairs on the back of Rosemary's neck stand on end. The clacking of Miranda's heels echoed faintly from deeper within the building, growing closer with each passing second.

"Quick," Rosemary hissed, grabbing her mother's arm and tugging her behind a large potted plant.

Miranda's silhouette paused at the end of the corridor, her head turning slightly as if sensing their presence. Rosemary held her breath, her grip tightening on Evelyn's arm. Her mother's perfume wafted around them, and she prayed it wouldn't give them away. But after what felt like an eternity, Miranda continued on, disappearing around a corner.

"Come on," Rosemary whispered, taking the lead and tiptoeing towards the stairwell.

As they crept up the stairs, Evelyn leaned close, her earlier terse demeanor softening slightly. "Is this how all your investigations proceed?" she murmured, "skulking about like common criminals?"

Rosemary paused, quirking an eyebrow at her mother. "Why yes, actually. Though I prefer to think of it as *gathering critical intelligence through covert means.*"

To her surprise, a small smile played at the corners of Evelyn's mouth. "How thrilling," she breathed, her eyes sparkling with an excitement Rosemary had never seen before. She blinked, momentarily taken aback.

Where was her prim and proper mother's usual distaste for anything unseemly? Nearing the top of the stairs, Rosemary pushed the thought aside, refocusing on the task at hand. Backs pressed against the wall, she and Evelyn crept down the darkened corridor, the only illumination a sliver of light peeking out from beneath a door at the opposite end.

Keeping out of sight, Rosemary strained to see around the corner to where Miranda stood before Eleanor's desk, her arms crossed and jaw clenched. Eleanor stiffened, her eyes wary when they met Miranda's gaze. Tension crackled between them as the pair engaged in a silent standoff.

Miranda's voice cut through the air, sharp and trembling. "I need to know. Is it true?"

"Is what true?" Eleanor finally asked, measured but cautious.

"Did you think I wouldn't find out?" Rosemary's heart tightened at the raw pain in her cousin's voice.

Hands shaking, Eleanor slowly rose from her chair. "Find out what, exactly?"

Miranda's eyes searched Eleanor's face. "About you and Charles. Did he ask you to go to New York with him?"

Eleanor's shoulders sagged slightly as she exhaled. "Charles did extend an invitation," she admitted, her voice steady but tinged with something Rosemary couldn't quite place.

The revelation struck Miranda like a physical blow, her breath hitching in her chest. For a moment, she looked as if she might crumble into a million pieces. But then, the fragility vanished, replaced by a hardness that straightened her back and clenched her jaw like a vise.

Rosemary leaned forward slightly, unwilling to miss a word. She could feel her mother shift beside her, no doubt reveling in the chance to overhear such a scintillating confrontation.

"He offered me a job, Miranda."

"A job? That's not what I've heard." Miranda spat out the words, her grief filling them with venomous suspicion. Rosemary watched intently, noting the devastation etched across Miranda's features. The pain in her eyes seemed to run deeper than simple jealousy.

Eleanor's voice was low and placating. "Miranda, please. Whatever you've heard—"

"There are rumors...people are saying there was more to it than that. Was there...was there something more between you two?" Evelyn's lips curled into a satisfied smile, and Rosemary couldn't help but find herself vexed by her mother's smug certainty.

"I hadn't thought you'd listen blindly to fools, Miranda." Bitter now, Eleanor's eyes flashed.

The tension between the two stretched taut as a wire. Miranda's face flushed with indignation, but she remained silent as though the words had lodged in her throat, choking out any possible response.

"Your accusations are baseless," Eleanor continued. "And to have them come from you is worse than hearing them from any gossip-mongering man on the floor."

"Baseless?" Miranda finally found her voice. "All of Woolridge & Sons suspects there was something between you two." She paused, letting the assertion hang in the air.

"I can't deny the rumors existed," Eleanor replied, her tone measured. "But that doesn't mean they were accurate. It was purely professional. He believed in my ideas and thought I could contribute in America. Charles wasn't like the others. He saw me as more than a pretty face or a set of legs to ogle."

"Let me be perfectly clear," Eleanor continued, her irritation simmering beneath the surface. "What Charles and I had was respect and professional camaraderie. Nothing more."

But Miranda cut her off, taking a step closer. "Don't lie to me, Eleanor. Not you." Miranda's outcry echoed against the high ceilings, and Rosemary tensed, alarmed by the growing agitation in her voice. Chest heaving with the force of her breaths, Miranda's cheeks flushed with a rosy hue that spoke of anger and something more.

Eleanor stepped back as if slapped, her facade of righteous indignation crumbling for a moment before her resolve visibly hardened. "Why is it so hard for you to believe he valued my opinion? That he thought I had something to offer beyond typing memos and fetching coffee? It seems you are blinded by your affections, unable to see the truth."

The retort sliced through Miranda, cutting deeper than any physical wound. She looked as though she might respond, her lips parting slightly, but no sound emerged.

Puzzled, Rosemary watched the scene unfold, the tension between the two women charged with more than just romantic rivalry. She couldn't shake the nagging sensation that she was missing crucial information. The raw vulnerability beneath Miranda's anger, the way her hands shook—suggested something deeper that didn't quite fit her mother's theory.

"I held Charles in high esteem." Eleanor's voice softened as she paused, noticing the flicker of hurt crossing Miranda's features. "He was one of the few true gentlemen I've had the privilege to know in this place. And contrary to the sordid tales that seem to titillate the masses, I assure you, there was no romantic entanglement in his offer. "

Miranda stared at Eleanor for a long moment until finally, her posture changed, her anger seeming to deflate slightly.

"Charles," Eleanor said, her voice a regretful echo in the sparsely furnished office, "treated everyone with respect...well, except for those who crossed a certain line."

"Like Jonathan Palmer?" Miranda guessed, her brow furrowing at the mention of the disgraced employee.

"Indeed," Eleanor replied, her eyes momentarily hardening. "Jonathan was the catalyst for so many unpleasant whispers. He spread vile rumors about Charles and me before his termination. Charles showed him the door because he was a blight on this establishment—a cad, through and through."

"Then why..." she began, her voice trailing off. She swallowed hard and tried again. "Why didn't you tell me about the offer?"

Confused by the question, Rosemary's brow furrowed. Why would Miranda care if Eleanor hadn't told her about a job offer? It struck her as odd, not fitting with the assumption that Miranda was jealous of Eleanor's relationship with Charles.

Eleanor's response only deepened Rosemary's bewilderment. "Because I wasn't going to take it," she said softly, her eyes never leaving Miranda's face. "I had my reasons for staying here."

Miranda stepped closer to Eleanor, her voice dropping to an urgent whisper. "But you have to take it. Don't you see? Offers like that don't come around all the time, not for us. You know I'm right."

Rosemary's eyes widened at the unexpected softness in Miranda's tone. Gone was the angry, sharp-tongued woman who had blown into the office in a fury. In her place stood someone vulnerable, almost pleading. It was as if a mask had slipped, revealing a depth of emotion Rosemary hadn't thought Miranda capable of.

"I can't just leave," Eleanor replied, her voice equally soft. "There are... complications."

Miranda reached out, her fingers brushing Eleanor's arm before falling away. "We could make it work. Together."

Rosemary's mind raced, piecing together the clues she'd overlooked. The realization hit Rosemary like a thunderbolt. The lingering glances, the unexplained tensions, Miranda's lack of interest in Desmond...suddenly, it all made sense. Miranda's eagerness to join the factory tour, her agitation when Eleanor wasn't there – it hadn't been about Charles at all. She'd been trying to see Eleanor, to steal a moment together away from prying eyes.

As she watched the two women stand close, their bodies angled towards each other like flowers seeking the sun, Rosemary felt a mixture of awe and embarrassment. How had she misread the situation so completely?

These women weren't rivals; they were lovers, or at the very least, desperately wanted to be.

Evelyn leaned in close, her brow furrowed in confusion. "I don't understand," she whispered. "Why are they acting so... familiar? Surely they can't be friends after all this fuss about Charles."

Rosemary suppressed a sigh, glancing at her mother's perplexed expression. Evelyn's worldview was as rigid as starched linen, with no room for the unconventional. "It's...complicated, Mother," she murmured, choosing her words carefully. "I think it's best we don't jump to conclusions."

"But it doesn't make any sense," Evelyn persisted, her voice barely audible.

"Shh," Rosemary hushed her, grateful for once for her mother's inability to conceive of such a relationship.

Rosemary tugged gently on her mother's sleeve. "Come on," she whispered. "Let's get out of here before we're discovered."

Eighteen

They crept from their hiding spot and into the stairwell, Evelyn still muttering under her breath about the peculiar behavior they'd witnessed. Rosemary guided her towards the reception booth, hulking like a shadowy monolith in the darkened office.

"I can't see a bloody thing," Rosemary muttered, fumbling in the dark. "How do we turn the lights on?"

"Your guess is as good as mine."

With a sigh, she continued her blind exploration, rummaging around until she hit upon a small desk lamp. When she switched it on, the pool of light illuminated a cluttered mess atop the desk - pens strewn about, scattered stacks of message slips, and what appeared to be a half-eaten sandwich - and cast long shadows over the cramped space, exaggerating the mess of cords spilling from the switchboard.

The stack of charity boxes still loomed in the corner, forcing Evelyn to twist awkwardly to avoid knocking them over. The booth's usual chaotic energy had been replaced with an unsettling silence. It felt like being in the belly of a machine that had temporarily gone to sleep. A light on the switchboard blinked once, catching Rosemary's eye.

"Do you know what any of these do?" she asked her mother, squinting at the switchboard covered in a dizzying array of buttons, sockets, and toggles.

"Heavens no, dear," Evelyn replied, peering over

Rosemary's shoulder. "Don't be ridiculous. I was counting on you to figure it out."

"I'm just as lost as you. I've never seen so many controls in my life. Lois really ought to label these properly."

She pressed one experimentally. Nothing happened.

"Maybe this one?" Evelyn suggested, jabbing at another button.

A loud buzz emanated from somewhere in the office, making them both jump.

"Good lord," Rosemary breathed. "What was that?"

"I haven't the foggiest," Evelyn replied. "But I'd rather not set off any more alarms."

As they sifted through the papers, Evelyn tsked disapprovingly. "Goodness, would you look at this? It's an absolute shambles."

Rosemary peered at the notepad Evelyn held up. Scribbled messages covered every inch, overlapping and barely legible. Names and numbers jumbled together with no discernible order. "Lois certainly isn't the tidiest receptionist, is she?"

"No wonder that girl can never keep anything straight. It's like a cyclone hit this desk."

Rosemary shuffled through the jumbled papers, squinting to decipher Lois's looping scrawl. "You're right; there's no rhyme or reason to any of it. Dates and names all willy-nilly."

"How on earth does she keep track of anything?" Rosemary wondered aloud. "It's as if she has no system whatsoever." She returned to shuffling through the stack of messages, hoping to spot some clue amidst the clerical catastrophe.

"It certainly causes one to wonder how she managed to secure the job in the first place," Evelyn mused.

A memory tickled at the back of Rosemary's mind. "You

know, Vera always says you should embellish your application. Perhaps Lois took that advice a bit too far?"

"Embellish? She fabricated entirely, more like. I can't imagine she listed 'utter disorganization' as one of her skills."

Just as Rosemary was about to give up hope, a particular slip caught her eye. "Mother, look at this! It says, 'Please call Lady Foxworthy to Father's office at 3 PM. Urgent.' It's from Miranda."

"From Miranda. How strange." Leaning over Rosemary's shoulder, her mother pointed out, "And the date matches the day Beatrice stopped by to drop off her check for the children's benefit."

"Why do you suppose Miranda would want Lady Foxworthy to come to the office?"

Evelyn's brow, which had been deeply furrowed, suddenly smoothed. She let out a chuckle. "I think I know what Miranda was up to. Playing a spot of matchmaker, I'd wager. She's always been keen on her father finding companionship after what happened with her mother."

"That would explain a lot," Rosemary agreed, tapping her chin. "It did seem rather obvious that Uncle Henry fancies Lady Foxworthy, although if you ask me, he couldn't handle her in the long term. If that was Miranda's plan, it certainly backfired spectacularly. Foiled by a rival suitor."

Evelyn's shoulders slumped. "Indeed. Your sister would call it poetic, but I'm afraid I have to disagree. It's almost cruel. Henry is the type of man Beatrice has always been able to wrap around her finger, often to their detriment." Her voice turned thoughtful. "Moths flying too close to a flame."

"You mean to say that he's the type she likes to keep under her thumb but would never truly commit to?"

"Precisely," Evelyn agreed, and Rosemary wondered if that was how her mother saw her relationship with Max.

As Rosemary set the message aside, her elbow knocked into a precariously balanced stack of boxes behind the reception desk. The tower toppled, spilling the contents across the floor in a cacophony of clatters and thumps.

"Blast it all!" Rosemary muttered, dropping to her knees to clean up the mess. She paused, however, when her fingers brushed against a supple leather surface. "Mother, you don't suppose...is this Charles's missing satchel?"

Evelyn crouched down beside her daughter, eyes widening in recognition. "It most certainly is. But what's it doing buried under all this lost and found rubbish?"

Together, they heaved the satchel from beneath the misplaced items. Rosemary's fingers trembled as she undid the clasps and retrieved a stack of papers and folders from inside, her eyes wide with curiosity as she flipped through the first few papers. "Unfortunately, it's all Greek to me."

Evelyn gently shoved Rosemary aside, her brow furrowed in concentration. Scanning through the papers with a keen eye, a frown began to tug at the corners of her mouth. "We need to show these to your father and Frederick."

Rosemary eyed the switchboard warily, its tangled cords mocking her technological ignorance. Instead, she turned to the simpler, more familiar black telephone resting on the edge of Lois's desk. With a relieved sigh, she lifted the receiver and dialed her brother's number on the rotary, her heart pounding in her chest as she waited for someone to pick up.

"Hello? Woolridge residence." Frederick's voice crackled through the line, slightly breathless and tinged with worry.

"Freddie, it's me. Mother and I have found something-"

But before she could continue, Frederick cut her off.

"Rosie, thank goodness you're all right. Listen, something's happened..."

"What is it?" A sense of foreboding washed over her. "There hasn't been another...death...has there?"

"No, nothing like that. It's just...well," Frederick hesitated momentarily as if gathering his thoughts. "Johnathan Palmer showed up at the house not long ago, raving like a madman. Said he needed to warn us about something."

Rosemary's eyes widened in shock. Johnathan Palmer, the prime suspect in Charles's murder, had come to Frederick and Vera's home. "Warn us? About what?"

"I don't know," he admitted, frustration evident in his tone. "He sounded barmy, at least as far as the police were concerned. It seems Max had a pair of constables stationed across the street. They chased Palmer off the property before he could get to the door, and now he's disappeared again."

Rosemary took a deep breath, clutching the phone tighter. "Frederick, listen carefully. We've found Charles's satchel filled with important-looking notes and files. Neither Mother nor I can decipher the details, but if this was the last thing Charles was working on before he died, we may have the evidence we need to find his killer."

Frederick's voice took on a note of determination. "Right. The three of you need to come home straight away. We'll figure out our next move together."

Rosemary frowned, confusion creeping into her voice. "What do you mean, 'the three of us'?"

"You, Mother, and Stella," Frederick replied just as warily.

"Stella's not with you?"

There was a moment of stunned silence on both ends of the line. Rosemary's heart began to race, her palms growing clammy as she gripped the receiver.

"She returned to the dining room just after I left you and Mother on the footway, grabbed her coat, and left again. We thought she was with you."

A cold dread settled in the pit of Rosemary's stomach. "No, Frederick. We thought she was with you at the house."

"Oh no," she whispered, more to herself than to Frederick. "Where could she be?"

As if in answer to Rosemary's whispered question, the red light on the telephone system began to blink insistently again. Rosemary's eyes widened, her heart skipping a beat.

She nudged Evelyn and pointed. "Do you think that means it's ringing?"

"I can't imagine what else it would mean," Evelyn said, rushing to the console and taking a closer look. "That one is labeled, at least. It's the dedicated line from the factory, but how do we answer it?"

"Frederick, I'll have to call you back," Rosemary said hurriedly. "There's another call coming in on the factory line."

Without thinking, she set the mouthpiece down to fumble with the unfamiliar switchboard, her fingers trembling as she tried to decipher which toggle to use. Evelyn leaned in, her brow furrowed with concern. "Perhaps one of those wires?"

"How on earth does Lois manage this contraption?" Rosemary muttered, reaching out to help.

"She doesn't."

Rosemary scanned the board, eventually spotting wire labeled "Factory Line." She reached for it hesitantly. "It can't be that complicated... Surely?" she muttered, picking up the headset and inserting the plug into the socket. The light stopped blinking, replaced by the faint hum of a live line.

"Hello? This is Rosemary at the reception desk," she said hesitantly.

There was a crackle of static before a hushed, familiar voice came through the telephone, barely above a whisper. "Rosemary? Oh, thank God. It's Stella."

Rosemary's heart leaped into her throat. "Stella? What's going on? We've been worried sick!"

"I followed you—or I thought I did. I'm at the factory," Stella whispered, her voice tight with fear. "And I'm in trouble."

Rosemary and her mother exchanged a look of growing horror. "What kind of trouble?" Evelyn demanded, leaning in closer to the receiver and mouthpiece. "Are you hurt?"

"No, not yet," Stella replied, her words coming out in a frantic rush. "But I overheard something...something terrible. I think..."

A sudden crash echoed through the line, followed by a sharp intake of breath. "Oh God, he's coming! I have to hide."

Evelyn, who had her ear pressed to the other side of the receiver, interjected, "Who, Stella? What's happening?"

There was a beat of silence, broken only by the sound of Stella's ragged breathing. "Rosemary, you need to listen carefully," she whispered at last, her voice barely audible over the crackling line. "He's going to burn it all down."

Nineteen

Rosemary pulled the receiver away from her ear, staring at it in disbelief as the line went dead.

"Burn the whole place down?" Evelyn exclaimed, her eyes wide with worry that was only a hair's breadth away from becoming sheer panic. "Who? What is she talking about?"

"Johnathan Palmer, I presume." Frederick's ominous warning echoed through Rosemary's mind. She tried to ring him back, to no avail. She took a steadying breath and turned to her mother with resolve burning in her eyes. "The line is occupied, and we've no time to waste. We have to get to the factory. Now."

As promised, Jensen waited at the curb with Lady Foxworthy's town car still running.

"Can you take us to Clerkenwell?" For once, Evelyn's voice was a plea, not a command. Hearing the urgency in her voice, the driver agreed without protest, and they sped off, racing against an unknown clock. "A doubly large tip," she said under her breath to Rosemary.

As the city blurred by outside the windows, Evelyn fretted, her hands twisting into knots in her lap. "Why on earth would she have gone there?"

Rosemary bit her lip, her mind working furiously to decipher Stella's fragmented explanation. "She must have taken a carriage taxi from the hotel and followed us. As far as why she went to the factory, your guess is as good as mine."

"This is all my fault. I should have let her come with us. Now look what's happened," she said miserably.

Rosemary's heart clenched at the sound of her mother's anguish. "Everything is going to be all right," she assured, not quite sure she believed the words herself. Dread settled like a lead weight in her stomach at the thought of her sister alone and vulnerable, trapped with a potential murderer.

Her mother was quiet for a long moment. "What does this Palmer fellow have to be so disgruntled about, anyway? He's found another position, after all."

"Perhaps he doesn't fancy working with a cad like Sam Drakeford. I can't imagine any of his employees are particularly satisfied." It was the first explanation that popped into Rosemary's head, giving her pause.

"Something doesn't add up," she murmured, her brow furrowed. "I don't think for one second Drakeford didn't know about the connection between Palmer and Woolridge & Sons, do you?"

"You think Drakeford could be involved somehow?" Evelyn's voice was tinged with uncertainty.

"Frederick said Johnathan was trying to warn us about something before the police chased him off. What if he's not the one behind all this?" Rosemary asked, nearly breathless.

"But why?"

"I don't know, but I can't shake the feeling that something doesn't fit," Rosemary admitted, frustration evident in her tone. "Motives are never as cut and dried as they seem in the crime pulps. It's not either love, money, or revenge; in real life, the reason people are driven to murder is almost always a combination of all three. What if Drakeford isn't the upstanding businessman he pretends to be?"

Evelyn considered the question. "Not everyone is as thorough as your father. It's possible he doesn't even know his entire staff by name. However, I find it highly unlikely that a man as put-together as he is would have overlooked such a connection. Particularly not during negotiations such as these, with a large sum of money on the line."

"A man as put-together as he is," Rosemary repeated, recalling Mr. Abernathy's comment about how Drakeford didn't quite belong amongst the upper crust despite looking and dressing the part. Both of their statements contradicted her own opinion of the man.

In Rosemary's estimation, Drakeford fell into the same category as her Uncle Henry, emitting something of a disheveled air. And yet, it occurred to her now that he'd only looked that way once—the first time she'd laid eyes on him, the morning of the factory tour shortly before discovering Charles's body.

Fragments of the macabre puzzle began to come together, coalescing into a clearer picture. Drakeford's shirt, she'd noticed at the time, hadn't matched the rest of his ensemble. True, it appeared the murderer got away clean, but one spot of blood was all it would have taken to necessitate a change of clothes. And his shoes, almost too pristine.

The realization hit Rosemary like a physical blow, stealing the breath from her lungs. Her hand flew to her mouth, stifling a gasp. "Oh my God," she breathed, her voice barely audible. "It's been Drakeford all along. He's the murderer." Rosemary explained her theory and the reasoning behind it. "If he had time to change his shirt, he had time to wipe off his shoes."

"You're right," Evelyn breathed, her voice barely above a

whisper. "I noticed, but I didn't think anything of it. "I just assumed he was in a hurry that morning."

"We have to find Stella," Evelyn said, her voice tight with urgency. "If Drakeford is behind this, there's no telling what he might do."

As they approached the factory, Rosemary's thoughts turned to Johnathan Palmer. He had tried to warn them, knowing the police were on his tail, risking his own safety to do so. And now, with the truth about Drakeford revealed, his actions made some sense. Palmer wasn't the enemy but an ally in a fight they hadn't even known they were waging.

"Look," Evelyn said as the car pulled to a stop, pointing up to where smoke billowed from the factory's stack. Rosemary scrambled out of the car, hurrying to keep pace with her mother's determined strides.

Inside, the cavernous space was eerily quiet, the usual hum of machinery conspicuously absent. The air hung heavy with the acrid scent of chemicals, and Rosemary's mind flashed back to Frederick's dire warning. If anyone tampered with the volatile substances stored there, the consequences could be catastrophic. Hearts pounding in unison, she and her mother made their way deeper into the labyrinth of machinery.

Evelyn opened her mouth to speak, but a sudden clatter from somewhere deep within the factory cut her off. Both women froze, their gazes locked on the darkened recesses of the building. Rosemary's heart hammered against her ribs as she strained to identify the source of the noise, every muscle in her body coiled tight with anticipation.

She scanned the shadows for any sign of movement, her ears straining for the slightest whisper of a response. They followed the sounds to the dye room, which spanned nearly two floors to accommodate the enormous vats. A series of platforms provided access to the upper section.

Suddenly, a loud hiss filled the air, followed by the clanking of gears. Rosemary and Evelyn ducked behind a large vat, peering around the edge to locate the source of the noise. There, in the center of the factory floor, was Sam Drakeford, his face illuminated by the glow from the fire he was stoking in one of the boiler furnaces.

"We were right," Rosemary whispered, her eyes wide with the realization. "And it looks as though he's trying to destroy evidence." His movements frantic, Drakeford muttered under his breath as he worked, and she knew without a doubt this was a man on the edge, desperate to cover his tracks at any cost.

Evelyn agreed, her hand shaking as she pointed to the handle of one of the valves. Set to a different position than the others, the pressure gauge climbed steadily, the needle edging towards the red zone. "He's planning to start a fire and make it look like an accident." Her hand shook when she

Blood pounding in her veins, Rosemary scanned the dye room, searching for any sign of her sister. Finally, she spotted Stella clinging to a pipe on a narrow platform high above the factory floor. Her face was streaked with tears, and she trembled in fear. Rosemary's breath caught in her throat as she realized the pipe pressed against her sister's cheek connected to the very boiler Drakeford tampered with.

"Mother," she hissed, pointing towards Stella. "We have to get her out of there, now. If that boiler gets too hot..."

She didn't need to finish the thought.

Evelyn peered up at her youngest daughter, her eyes darting to and fro, calculating the distance. "I can get to her," she said decisively. "You create a distraction."

"Are you certain? It looks dangerous, and you're..."

Her expression soured. "I'm what, Rosemary?"

"Nothing," Rosemary whispered, holding her hands up in surrender. "Have it your way. You get Stella; I'll handle Drakeford."

With a quick squeeze of Rosemary's hand, Evelyn slipped away, disappearing into the shadows. After a long moment, she reappeared at the bottom of the ladder leading to the catwalk. Rosemary watched as her mother hiked up her skirt, waiting until she'd begun to climb before stepping out from between the dye vats.

"Mr. Drakeford?" she called out, affecting a breathy voice and widening her eyes innocently, hoping to appeal to any ounce of chivalry the deranged businessman might still possess. "What are you doing here?"

He whirled, his expression going slack with shock before his lips turned into a sneer. "What are *you* doing here? It's Christmas Eve."

"This is my father's factory, after all. I have a right to be here." Rosemary added a waver to her voice, but Drakeford appeared skeptical.

"You can cut the innocent act. I'm no fool," he snapped, adding insult to what she hoped wouldn't turn out to be serious injury. She knew her acting skills wouldn't win any awards, but nevertheless, Rosemary thought she'd learned a little something from Vera.

To keep him talking, she complied with his request, squaring her shoulders and speaking gently but at her normal timbre. "It was you, wasn't it?"

It took every bit of Rosemary's self-control not to turn and run or at least back up a step when his head whipped up, and he all but snarled at her.

"Why, Mr. Drakeford?" she asked, her voice trembling

slightly. This time, it wasn't an act. "Why did you do it? What could possibly be worth all of this?"

He let out a harsh laugh. "You wouldn't understand," he spat. "You've never had to fight for anything in your life. You've never known what it's like to be on the brink of losing everything."

As he spoke, Rosemary's eyes darted to the pressure gauge, and she swallowed hard, knowing time was running out to save Stella—and possibly for any of them to get out alive.

Above them, Evelyn inched her way along the catwalk, her progress agonizingly slow. The metal groaned beneath her feet, threatening to give way at any moment while Stella still clung to the pipe, her face pale with terror.

Rosemary forced herself to focus on Drakeford, to keep him talking. "It doesn't have to be this way," she said, her voice soft and persuasive. "You can still make things right."

For a moment, he hesitated, a flicker of uncertainty crossing his face. But then his expression hardened, and he shook his head and growled, "No. It's too late for that."

She couldn't let him get to the boiler, couldn't let him finish what he'd started. The heat from the furnace was intense, the air shimmering with it.

"Mr. Drakeford, please," she pleaded, holding up her hands in a placating gesture. "This isn't who you are. I know you're a good man, deep down. You don't have to do this."

Drakeford's eyes were wild, his face contorted with rage and desperation. "You don't know anything about me," he snarled. "You and your perfect family, your perfect life."

"I know you've made mistakes," Rosemary said, her voice trembling. "But you can still be the man your father wanted you to be. The man I know you can be."

Drakeford's eyes flashed with a mix of desperation and

resentment. "You think it's that easy? You've never had to face real adversity. You've grown up with a silver spoon in your mouth."

Rosemary's gaze darted between her mother and sister above and Drakeford's accusatory stare. She swallowed hard, trying to maintain her composure. "So did you. Your father was a successful businessman, too. That can be a lot of pressure."

While he talked, she edged closer to the valve, the heat from the boiler intensifying, causing beads of sweat to form on her brow and making it difficult to breathe. Her heart pounded in her chest, but she refused to let her fear show. She had to keep his attention focused on her, giving Evelyn the time she needed to reach Stella.

"You don't know what you're talking about," Sam scoffed, his voice rising. "Your family is lucky. Everything just falls into place for you."

"It wasn't luck. It was hard work. My father built his business from the ground up, just like yours did."

Sam laughed bitterly. "It takes more than just hard work, Rosemary. Your father made more than good decisions. He was bold in the right ways. There's a fine line between success and failure, and being a good person doesn't always have anything to do with it."

Evelyn was now mere feet from Stella, the heat from the pipes reddening her cheeks and drawing beads of moisture to her brow.

Drakeford ran a hand through his hair, his eyes growing distant. "I should have paid more attention and learned from him. But I'm not my father. I'm not yours, and I'm not Frederick." His gaze snapped back to Rosemary, a desperate gleam in his eye. "But I thought I could save my business by hitching my ride to Cecil. I thought I could turn it all around."

"I understand, Sam. The pressure to succeed, to live up to expectations. But this isn't the way."

Drakeford's face contorted, a war raging behind his eyes. For a moment, Rosemary thought she saw a flicker of the man he once was, the man he could be again. But then his expression hardened, a chilling resolve settling over him.

"You're wrong. It is too late. For all of us."

Rosemary's heart sank at the finality in Drakeford's tone. She glanced up at her mother, who had reached the end of the catwalk. She stretched out her hand, fingers straining towards Stella.

"What do you mean?" Rosemary asked, her voice steady despite the fear coursing through her veins as she hoped against hope that he felt the need to unburden himself.

Drakeford's shoulders slumped, the fight draining out of him. "Charles was too smart, too observant. He discovered that I had altered my books and made myself look like a viable investor when, in reality, I had squandered my father's fortune. My business was on the verge of bankruptcy."

He began to pace, his hands trembling. "When Johnathan came looking for a job, I saw an opportunity. He said Woolridge & Sons was sound and that, with the right investment, it could thrive. So, I leveraged everything I had left to go in on this deal. But now, even that is lost."

Rosemary's mind raced, trying to piece together the events of that fateful day. "What happened when you arrived at the factory, Sam? The truth, this time."

Drakeford stopped pacing, his eyes haunted. "I lied about the back door being locked. I arrived early, just like Abernathy, and found Charles there, smoking a cigarette. He let me in, and as we walked towards R&D, he asked about my files and my finances."

A shudder ran through him, and he closed his eyes. "I panicked. I thought he knew about the cooked books, that he would expose me. I couldn't take that chance, couldn't lose everything. So I..."

His voice trailed off, the unspoken words hanging heavy in the air. Rosemary's stomach turned, the pieces clicking into place with sickening clarity. Above them, Evelyn reached for Stella, the platform bowing under the extra weight.

Drakeford's voice trembled as he continued, "I tried to reason with Charles, but he wouldn't listen. He said he was going to tell Cecil everything and reevaluate our business relationship. I just...I snapped."

His gaze fell to his hands as if seeing the blood that once stained them. "I grabbed the first thing I could find from a nearby workbench—a broken weaving shuttle and...I killed him. I knew immediately that I had made a terrible mistake, that I was in too deep. But it was too late."

Rosemary fought back the wave of revulsion that threatened to overwhelm her, forcing herself to maintain a calm facade. "And then you changed your shirt—that's why it didn't match your suit," she finished for him.

Drakeford nodded. "Fortunately, I had a spare in the car. I cleaned my shoes and tried to make it look like I had just arrived."

As his confession spilled forth, Evelyn balanced precariously on the narrow beam, the metal creaking ominously beneath her feet. Stella, her face streaked with tears, reached out desperately, her delicate hands grasping at the air.

Evelyn steadied herself and took a cautious step forward. The beam swayed dangerously, threatening to pitch her into the vat below. Another step, and then another.

Rosemary watched in horror as her mother teetered on the

edge of the platform, unable to suppress the gasp that escaped her lips when Evelyn bent her knees and leaped across the gap.

For a moment, she seemed to hang suspended in the air but then, with a jarring impact, landed hard beside Stella. The beam behind her collapsed into the inferno below, drawing Drakeford's attention. His gaze snapped up just in time to witness the daring rescue, the flicker of surprise that crossed his features quickly replaced by a snarl of rage.

He lunged forward, his hands outstretched, but Rosemary was ready for him. She sidestepped his attack, using his own momentum to send him stumbling past her. Drakeford whirled around, his eyes wild with fury.

Seizing the moment of distraction, Rosemary stepped forward, her heart pounding in her chest. She recalled the self-defense lessons she'd taken with the rest of the Ladies for London Vitality, the movements suddenly crystal clear in her mind. With a swift, decisive motion, she delivered a well-aimed strike to Drakeford's chest, knocking him off balance.

Stumbling backward, his arms flailed as he tried to regain his footing, but it was too late. With a heavy thud, he hit the ground, banging his head hard enough on the floor to stun him into stillness.

Rosemary turned her attention to the boiler; the pressure gauge deep in the red zone. A shrill whistle pierced the air, signaling the imminent danger. Her eyes scanned the machinery, searching for the release valve.

There! She spotted it dangerously close to the flames. Gritting her teeth, Rosemary grabbed a discarded cloth, wrapping it around her hand for protection. The heat was intense, the fire licking at her skin as she reached for the valve.

"Come on, come on," she urged, her fingers straining to turn the metal wheel. It resisted at first, the years of grime and rust making it nearly impossible to move. But Rosemary refused to give up, pouring all her strength into the effort.

With a sudden hiss, the valve began to turn, steam escaping in a deafening rush. Rosemary cranked it open, the pressure releasing just as the boiler threatened to explode. The whistle died away, replaced by the steady roar of the flames just as the factory doors burst open, and Max strode in, his face a mask of determination. Rosemary whirled around, her heart flooding with relief at the sight of him. "Max! How did you—"

"Frederick," Max said, his gaze sweeping the scene. "He heard everything through the phone. Sent me right over." His eyes landed on Drakeford, who lay unconscious on the floor. "Looks like you ladies had things well in hand."

Rosemary managed a shaky laugh. "You could say that." She glanced up at the platform, where Evelyn and Stella still clung to each other, their faces etched with fear and exhaustion. "But we need to get them down. The pipe..."

Max followed her gaze, his brow furrowing. "I'll radio for backup. We'll have them down in no time." He crossed to Drakeford, slipping on handcuffs before hauling him upright. "As for this one, he's got a lot to answer for."

TWENTY

The morning sun shined through the frosted windowpanes, casting a warm glow across Stella's face as she sat nestled in the plush armchair, a steaming cup of tea cradled in her hands. Cheerful voices drifted in from the entrance hall, and she sat up straighter, straining to hear. Watching from across the room, Rosemary could almost hear her sister wondering, *Could it be...?*

Suddenly, the door burst open, and in bounded Nelly, his cheeks flushed from the cold, eyes sparkling with merriment. Leonard followed closely behind, little Lyn bundled in his arms, his grey wool coat dusted with a sprinkling of snow.

To Rosemary's surprise, Miranda stepped in behind them, looking chic as always in her crimson cloche hat.

"Merry Christmas, Mother!" Nelly cried, flinging his arms around Stella in a tight hug.

Stella inhaled her son's familiar scent, joy and astonishment written all over her face. Rosemary knew her sister had resigned herself to spending a quiet holiday at Frederick and Vera's without her husband and children. And yet, here they were—a Christmas miracle delivered right to their doorstep.

"What a wonderful surprise!" Stella exclaimed, blinking back happy tears as she embraced Lyn and Leonard in turn. "However did you manage it?"

"We drove through the night," Leonard explained, unbuttoning his coat. "The storm finally let up around midnight. We thought we'd arrive in time for Christmas breakfast but it seems we missed it!"

"No matter, you're here now," Stella said, beaming. "It's the best gift I could ask for. But wait - where's Uncle Henry?" She glanced at Miranda questioningly. A sly smile played at the corners of her cousin's lips.

"Don't you worry, he'll be along," Miranda said with a wink. "Father has impeccable timing."

"In the meantime, why don't we see what father and the boys have cooked up in the kitchen, hmm?" Rosemary suggested, a mischievous glint in her eye.

As if on cue, a loud crash sounded from the vicinity of the kitchen, followed by muffled curses and clanging pots. Stella grimaced. When Frederick made a comment about the fluffiness of her scrambled eggs at breakfast, Vera had suggested—insisted, really—that the men take charge of Christmas dinner this year while the women enjoyed a peaceful moment.

For the entertainment value alone, Rosemary backed Vera up, and so did Stella. Surprisingly, Evelyn only put up a token protest. But from the sound of things, that peace was in jeopardy.

Cecil poked his head through the doorway, his hair askew and an apron tied haphazardly around his waist.

"Ah, I thought I heard the dulcet tones of familial joy," he said sardonically. "Leonard, Miranda, lovely to see you, truly. Now if you'll excuse me, I must get back to my flambé before Max sets the house ablaze."

"Are you sure you lot don't need any help?" Stella asked, trying to keep a straight face at the sight of the usually unflappable Cecil so out of sorts. "It sounds rather...lively in there." Little Nelly looked on with interest but continued to snuggle with his mother, pressing his chubby pink cheeks into Stella's neck. Rosemary noticed Vera watching him with soft eyes.

"No, no, we have it all under control," Cecil insisted, although the wild look in his eyes suggested otherwise.

Frederick appeared at Cecil's elbow then, a smudge of flour on his nose and gravy splattered down his front.

"Under control?" he sputtered. "The goose is still raw in the middle, the potatoes are a gluey mass, and I'm fairly certain Max just used salt instead of sugar in the pudding!"

"It's a work in progress!" Cecil insisted. "Rome wasn't built in a day, and neither is Christmas dinner!"

With that, the two men retreated back to the kitchen, their bickering growing fainter as the door swung shut behind them.

Stella shared an amused glance with her sister before turning back to her family, determined to soak up every minute with them, culinary disasters be damned. Nelly had finally become distracted, crawling around near the tree, examining the brightly wrapped parcels curiously. Miranda had procured a crystal decanter of sherry and was pouring generous glasses.

Rosemary watched Stella sink back into her armchair, Leonard's steady hand coming to rest on her shoulder, her face reflected deep contentment. With her loved ones surrounding her and the promise of her Uncle Henry's imminent arrival, it was already shaping up to be a perfectly imperfect Christmas. Just the way it was meant to be.

"So, what's everyone planning for New Year's Eve?" Rosemary asked, sipping her sherry. "I assume we're all getting together again?"

A loud clatter sounded from the kitchen, followed by muffled cursing. Frederick poked his head out, his face flushed. "At this rate, we'll still be cooking Christmas dinner come New Year's!"

Just then, the doorbell rang, and Miranda leaped up to answer it, returning moments later wearing a beaming smile. "Look who's here!" she announced.

Henry strode into the room, decked out in a full Santa Claus costume, complete with a fluffy white beard and a sack slung over his shoulder. "Ho ho ho!" he bellowed, his eyes twinkling. "Merry Christmas, everyone!"

Nelly squealed with delight, rushing over to hug him. Henry laughed, lifting him up and spinning him around. Hardly more than an infant, Lyn merely stared at him from her mother's lap while the adults watched the scene with fond smiles, caught up in the festive moment.

As everyone tore into their gifts, Cecil told the story of Stella's first Christmas and how Lionel had complained that he hadn't wanted a sister, insisting he'd rather have had a puppy.

In the midst of the merriment, Frederick suddenly sniffed the air, his eyes widening. "Do you smell that?" he asked, his voice laced with panic.

A beat of silence followed before Cecil bolted for the kitchen, Frederick and Max hot on his heels. They returned moments later, their faces ashen.

"The goose," Frederick said numbly. "It's burnt to a crisp."

"And the pudding," Max added, holding up a blackened lump. "I fear it's beyond salvation."

For a moment, everyone stared at the ruined dishes, the weight of the culinary disaster sinking in. Then, slowly, a chuckle escaped from Stella's lips. It spread to Miranda, then Rosemary, until the entire room was filled with laughter.

"Well," Stella said, wiping tears of mirth from her eyes, "it looks like we'll be having an unconventional Christmas feast this year."

"All right," Frederick said said. "You've made your point."

"What, Freddie?" Rosemary asked innocently, "I would have thought that surely three capable men such as yourselves would have no trouble preparing a single meal for the family."

Evelyn smirked. "What was that you were saying earlier, darling? That cooking is no more difficult than arithmetic?"

"And did I not hear one of you claim that any man worth his salt could whip up a feast fit for a king?" Rosemary chimed in loudly, her eyes sparkling.

Cecil emerged from the kitchen, his apron now stained with what appeared to be cranberry sauce. "I may have underestimated the complexity of the task at hand," he admitted grudgingly.

Evelyn said, shaking her head. "Perhaps this will teach you to have a bit more empathy for poor Lois and her struggles with the switchboard."

Stella's eyes sparkled as she turned to the group. "I have an idea. Why don't we call Lady Foxworthy and see if she can squeeze us in at the Grand Lion? Perhaps we can actually finish a meal there this time."

Rosemary opened her mouth to respond but was interrupted by the sound of the front door closing.

"That won't be necessary, my lady."

All eyes turned to see Wadsworth entering the room, his arms laden with bags and boxes. He looked up, a smile spreading across his face as he took in the scene before him.

"Merry Christmas, everyone," he said warmly, setting down his burdens. "I hope I'm not interrupting anything."

"Wadsworth, you devil!" Vera exclaimed, rushing over to deposit a loud peck on his cheek. "Aren't you supposed to be spending the holidays with your family?"

Rosemary's butler smiled. "Well, I was, but then I received a call from Miss Gladys. She discovered you'd all been left to your own devices and requested my assistance." He gestured to the bags and boxes. "She thought it might be a bit much for you ladies to handle after your harrowing experience at Woolridge & Sons and took the liberty of arranging a feast fit for the occasion."

"You're an absolute angel, darling. Thank you."

"I'm merely the courier. It is Gladys you should thank for the cooking."

As the group gathered around to investigate the contents of the bags, Frederick shifted uncomfortably, his eyes darting between Wadsworth and Vera. He cleared his throat, drawing their attention.

"I have a confession to make," he began, his voice hesitant. "I haven't been entirely truthful with you, darling."

Vera's brows furrowed in confusion. "What do you mean, Freddie?"

Frederick took a deep breath. "I've been commandeering Wadsworth to help me get settled in the new house. I may have had him come by and tidy up a few times. I'm sorry, I should have been honest."

After a moment of silence, Vera burst out laughing. "Oh, Frederick," she said, shaking her head in amusement. "You could have just told me. It isn't as though I would have minded."

Frederick's shoulders sagged in relief. "I know you wouldn't because you're the perfect wife. I just...I didn't want you to think I couldn't handle things on my own."

Vera reached out and took his hand, squeezing it gently. "Darling, I know you can handle things. But there's no shame in asking for help when you need it. Especially once the baby comes."

A collective gasp filled the room. Evelyn's eyes widened, her mouth falling open in shock. "Baby?" she repeated, her voice a mix of surprise and delight. "You're...you're having a baby?"

Vera nodded, a radiant smile spreading across her face. "Yes, we are. We were going to wait until after the holidays to tell everyone, but I suppose the cat's out of the bag now."

No wonder Vera had been so absent these past few days, Rosemary realized. She'd been pondering her great announcement. "I'm sorry, Rosie," Vera said, noticing her friend's expression. "I intended to tell you first, but things have been so...you know."

Rosemary opened her mouth to reassure Vera, but her father interjected. "Speaking of recent events," he said, turning towards his brother with a gleam in his eye. "I have a proposition for you, Henry. How would you feel about taking over as head of our American division?"

Henry blinked, his brows knitting together in confusion. "I don't know what to say," he stammered, his gaze darting between Cecil and Frederick. "I'm flattered, of course, but...are you sure I'm the right person for the job?"

Cecil frowned, leaning forward in his seat. "Why wouldn't you be? You've been with the company for years, and you've proven yourself time and time again."

Henry shook his head, a rueful smile tugging at his lips. "I appreciate the vote of confidence, Cecil, but I've never thought of myself as leadership material. I'm the chap you'd rather have behind the scenes. That's why I didn't put myself up for the job."

As the conversation continued, something clicked in

Rosemary's mind. The hushed conversation she and Stella had overheard between Henry and Miranda before the charity event... it wasn't about Charles's job at all. It was about Henry stepping into the role of Santa

She felt Miranda's gaze on her from across the room, and when Rosemary met it, she smiled warmly. She'd misjudged Henry, assuming the worst when in reality, he had been grappling with his own insecurities and doubts. She'd misjudged Miranda, too. Neither were mistakes she planned to make again.

Cecil leaned back, his expression thoughtful as he regarded Henry. "I didn't ask if you thought you deserved the job, Henry. I asked if you wanted it."

Henry looked towards Miranda, who nodded. He drew in a deep breath, squaring his shoulders as he turned back to Cecil. "You know what? I do. Always have. Miranda and I could certainly use a fresh start, and this opportunity...it feels like a sign."

A slow smile spread across Cecil's face, and he clapped Henry on the shoulder. "Then the job is yours, brother. And if you don't believe you deserve it, I'll just have to believe it enough for the both of us."

Henry chuckled. "I'll do my best to live up to your expectations, Cecil. I promise."

As the conversation shifted to the logistics of the move and the transition, his expression grew somber. "There's one thing, though. I know Charles had some strong feelings about...certain employees. I want to honor his wishes, so I won't try to hire Palmer back. But I would like to bring Eleanor Thornton with me. She's an invaluable asset to the company, and I couldn't imagine doing this without her."

Henry's eyes met his daughter's across the room, a moment

of weighted emotion passing between them. Affection for her uncle swelled even further as Rosemary studied Henry's face. He knew. He knew about Miranda and Eleanor's relationship, and he supported them.

The guests bid their farewells, leaving the Woolridge family alone in the aftermath of the eventful day. Evelyn sank onto the sofa, her mind whirling with the revelations of the past few hours. Frederick plopped down beside her, a mischievous glint in his eye.

"I must say, Mother, I'm impressed," he said, his tone deceptively casual. "I never pegged you as the open-minded type, but you seemed remarkably progressive in your response to Miranda and Eleanor's relationship."

Evelyn's brow furrowed. "Whatever do you mean, Frederick? They're colleagues and friends, are they not?"

"Oh, they're more than just friends, Mother. Much more." Frederick chuckled, shaking his head.

Evelyn stared at her son, uncomprehending.

"You mean to tell me...Miranda and Eleanor...they're..." Evelyn sputtered, her cheeks flushing crimson.

Frederick grinned, clearly enjoying his mother's discomfort. "In love? Yes, I believe that's the word you're looking for.

The grin fell right off his face when his mother's eyes rolled back in her head, and, in a performance even more dramatic than Lady Foxworthy's, she fainted dead away.

The next book, A Case of Luck and Death is available now from your favorite book retailer. Keep reading for a preview of the free novella you'll get for joining my newsletter.
~Also Available in Audiobook & Paperback Editions~

QUICK AUTHOR'S NOTE

Hi, I'm Emily and I write intriguing mysteries wrapped in a layer of proper English snark. I live in Maine, USA with my boyfriend, cat, chocolate lab...and too many books to count. *And if you're not careful, I might just kill you off in one of my novels...*

But seriously, the inspiration for Rosemary Lillywhite came to me on a quiet afternoon while leafing through an old family photo album. Among the sepia-toned images was a photograph of a poised woman with an enigmatic smile, surrounded by an air of timeless grace. She was a mystery herself—her story half-whispered in family lore and half-forgotten over generations. It made me wonder: what if a woman like her had secrets of her own, secrets she unraveled one thread at a time while solving mysteries?

From there, Rosemary began to take shape—smart, determined, and with an innate ability to see what others might overlook. She embodies the elegance of a bygone era and the tenacity of a modern sleuth, blending the best of both worlds.

Writing Rosemary has been a joy, and I hope you find her adventures as captivating as I do.

Thank you for joining her on this journey!

I'd love to offer you the chance to sign up for my newsletter—the best place to get new release updates, sales notifications, and other fun content.

Sign up, and as a thank-you gift for hanging out with me, you'll also get a FREE novella that isn't available anywhere else. And of course, I promise not to SPAM your inbox!

Love, hugs, and happy reading,

~Emily Queen~

P.S. If you enjoyed this book please consider leaving a review at your favorite store, Goodreads, or Bookbub. Your reviews help indie authors reach new readers!

Excerpt from *A Case of Luck & Death*

Rosemary Lillywhite felt the leather band tighten around her ankles and yank, hard, wrenching her sideways. Equilibrium lost, she heard blood rush to her ears as panic set in and her arms flailed in a wild attempt to avoid the length of wrought iron on a collision course with her temple.

Out of sheer reflex, she managed to pivot and grab hold of the would-be weapon, using it to steady herself rather than careening into it. The stair rail—a remnant from the townhouse's Victorian construction—terminated in a decorative wrought iron fleur-de-lis finial that Rosemary had always considered more hazardous than handsome.

"Dash, are you trying to do me in?" she called out at a volume at least two octaves higher than would have been considered polite in the sleepy London neighborhood, even in the afternoon.

The little dog merely stared up at Rosemary innocently while she untangled herself from the offending leather lead attached to his collar—a necessity given his penchant for dashing off to make merry in the streets should her grip loosen and he get away. White fur fluffed around his fox-like face, and his pointed ears twitched forward with interest. Despite weighing no more than a well-fed cat, Dash possessed the confidence of a mastiff and the mischief of a whole pack of terriers.

Having already enjoyed his morning constitutional, he was eager for his next adventure and, to illustrate the point, began wagging his plumed tail and glancing down the footway with mounting excitement.

"I know you want to go see Freddie and Vera, but I won't be able to walk you at all with two broken legs, will I?"

Before she could lead the mischievous dog towards their usual route, a question rang out from the steps next door. "Are you quite all right, Rose?"

Rosemary stiffened slightly at the voice using her nickname with such familiarity, but adroitly stifled a sigh and forced her face into a convivial expression as she turned towards her neighbor and former friend, Abigail Redberry. "Yes, thank you, but only just."

"Well, there isn't a more adorable menace in all of Marylebone." Abigail's smile didn't reach any closer to her eyes than Rosemary's had, but before the conversation could become even more uncomfortable, the Redberrys' front door opened and out spilled a heavily muscled man wearing blue overalls and carrying a tall armload of paint tins.

Dash barked at him with the same fervor he'd displayed towards every worker coming and going from the Redberrys' all week. The little dog's yapping had become as much a part of the neighborhood soundtrack as the hammering itself.

The worker tipped his head politely in their direction, the motion causing the stack of tins to tilt precariously. Rosemary winced, envisioning the spectacular, colorful crash, but the man righted the wayward pile with a fluid grace that suggested this wasn't his first dance with gravity. He resettled them against his chest and lumbered off around the corner as if nothing out of the ordinary had happened, Dash's barking following him down the street.

"My apologies," Abigail said when he'd gone. "I've asked the workmen to use Martin's office entrance, but it seems some of the materials won't fit that way. They should be finished before long, and we'll be out of your way. For good."

"Well, the neighborhood certainly won't be the same without you." Rosemary's words dripped with sincerity, but she was grateful Abigail had never known her well enough to detect the hint of relief in her tone.

Relations between the two had been strained since Abigail insinuated that Rosemary might be responsible for a murder that occurred a few months prior. In actuality, Rosemary had been the one to solve the crime, nearly becoming a victim herself in the process. Despite Abigail's attempted apology—and the fact that a small part of Rosemary couldn't blame her for wondering—the budding friendship had fizzled faster than a youthful infatuation.

Now, Rosemary could hardly wait for the couple to move on, although the adage of 'better the devil you know' was not lost on her. Whoever moved in next might very well make her vehemently wish for the Redberrys' return.

"Have a lovely time on your walk," Abigail called as Rosemary inched away with a helpless gesture towards Dash, who had reached the end of the lead and was clearly anxious to begin his afternoon stroll.

And a lovely afternoon it was; sunny and warm, the air perfumed by wallflowers that spilled over window boxes up and down Park Road. It had been storming on and off lately—that time of year, spring in London—and it was a nice change to be dry for once. Still, Rosemary was only able to enjoy the weather for a street or so before Dash stopped dead in his tracks and began to growl. His lips curled up to bare his teeth in what he must have believed a menacing snarl, but given he was mostly fur and excitement, the gesture only brought a wry smile to Rosemary's face.

She followed his glare to a large bay window where stood an enormous black cat, staring back at Dash with its fur puffed out every which way. They passed this block of flats often on their walks—it was the quickest route to Frederick and Vera's—and the cat was always there, though today it looked considerably thinner than usual, leading Rosemary to wonder if there were two nearly identical cats living at the same address.

"Let's press on, now," she coaxed, her attempts to lead the dog further down the street proving ineffective.

Dash continued his territorial display, yapping with increasing volume until the cat hissed back through the glass.

A woman appeared in the doorway, silver hair escaping from what had once been a neat bun, a pair of reading glasses dangling from a chain around her neck. Despite the warm weather, she wore a thick cardigan buttoned to her chin. As many times as Dash had tormented the cat through the glass, this was the first time Rosemary had seen its owner.

"Desdemona, you naughty thing!" the woman called out just as the black cat shot past her through the open door, hissing and spitting as she streaked across the small front garden towards Dash.

The woman chased after the cat briefly before it darted behind a rosebush and crouched there, tail twitching with indignation.

The woman turned to Rosemary with bright, intelligent eyes. "I do apologize for the commotion. Desdemona has particularly strong opinions about canines, I'm afraid—especially now, with kittens to protect."

"No harm done," she assured, though Dash continued to strain against his lead, clearly invested in continuing the standoff. Kittens would explain the cat's altered appearance, Rosemary realized as she observed Desdemona more closely—her belly appeared noticeably smaller than before, and her teats were visibly swollen with milk.

"I'm Eva. Eva Hanson Schweitzer," the woman said, extending an ink-stained hand. "And you must be the neighbor I've heard so much about. The one with the charming little dog who causes such delightful chaos of a morning."

Was Dash infamous for his barking? Rosemary wondered with some chagrin, then found herself smiling despite her intention to keep the exchange brief. "Rosemary Lillywhite, and this troublemaker is Dash."

"Wonderful! You simply must come in for tea," Eva announced, clasping her hands together with the enthusiasm of someone who'd just solved a particularly vexing puzzle. "I insist."

"Oh, that's very kind, but I really should—"

"Nonsense!" Eva waved away Rosemary's protest with remarkable authority for such a slight woman. "I won't take no for an answer. Besides, I've been dying to meet you properly."

Before Rosemary could mount another polite refusal, Eva had gently picked up the cat and was halfway inside, clearly expecting compliance. "Come along then! The kettle's just boiled." Indeed, the sound of its whistle wafted from within.

Rosemary's mother's voice echoed in her head with the sort of clarity earned by years of relentless drilling: One must always be gracious when invited for tea, Rosemary. It's the height of rudeness to refuse. She'd have liked nothing more than to ignore Evelyn Woolridge's permanently seared lessons in propriety, but they were as much a part of her as her own bones.

"That's very kind of you." The words came out before

Rosemary could stop them, following Eva through the front door with Dash trotting obediently at her heels.

Even though the little dog settled himself politely by the door, his eyes tracked Desdemona's every movement, while the cat's amber gaze remained fixed on him with the extreme suspicion usually reserved for known criminals. The tension between them was palpable—a canine-feline détente that could shatter at any moment.

Desdemona stalked regally across the room and disappeared behind a tall bookshelf where soft mewing suggested her kittens waited. Dash's head tilted at the sound, his tail giving a tentative wag before he seemed to think better of following.

Rosemary turned her attention to the flat, which could have been described either as a bibliophile's paradise or nightmare, depending on one's perspective. Books towered in precarious stacks on every available surface, and the air hung thick with the scents of old paper and strong tea. She caught sight of at least one volume with ornate Cyrillic script on its spine, wedged between what appeared to be a treatise on astronomy and a well-thumbed cookery book.

"Do you take milk? Sugar? Both?" Eva bustled about a tiny kitchen partially hidden behind a rounded archway. The gentle clatter of porcelain accompanied her voice, but she'd already moved on before Rosemary could answer. "You know, I've been watching the neighborhood for weeks now, and you're the first person who's walked past twice in the same day wearing different shoes."

Eva appeared in the archway, teapot in hand, studying Rosemary with the intensity of a scientist examining a particularly interesting specimen. "You're going somewhere special, aren't you? You have that look—the one that says you've planned your entire ensemble around the final destination rather than the journey."

"We—my friend Vera and I—are going to the theater in the park this evening."

"Oh!" Eva's eyes lit up with delight. "I'm going as well!"

The doorbell's sharp chime interrupted whatever Eva would have said next and sent every hair on Dash's back standing at attention. He scrambled up into Rosemary's lap, though he remained admirably silent—a small miracle, given his usual vocal protests to unexpected visitors. Desdemona reappeared, looking rather put out at the latest interruption, yet seemingly unable to resist investigating.

"Door's open!" Eva called out cheerfully, continuing to fuss with the tea service as if inviting perfect strangers into one's home was the most natural thing in the world. Rosemary could practically hear her mother's horrified gasp echoing all the way from Pardington.

The front door creaked, followed by tentative footsteps on the hardwood. A thin, grey-haired man appeared in the doorway, wire spectacles perched precariously on his nose and nervous energy radiating from every inch of his spare frame. He clutched something small and brown in his left hand—a rabbit's foot, Rosemary realized with an internal quirk of her eyebrow.

"Mr. Pembridge!" Eva beamed as though she'd been expecting him all along, and perhaps she had. "Do come in."

The man—Pembridge—practically vibrated with anxiety, his free hand fidgeting with his spectacles while a worn leather satchel hung from his shoulder. "Mrs. Schweitzer, I do hope I'm not intruding, but you did say—"

"Nonsense!" Eva gestured towards Rosemary with the sort

of theatrical flourish usually reserved for stage introductions. "I was just having tea with my new friend here. You're quite welcome to join us."

She darted back to the kitchen, returned, and pressed a cup into Pembridge's trembling hands then tapped the rabbit's foot. "Now then, what's this all about?"

Pembridge flushed scarlet. "I just thought it prudent, you know, on a day like today—"

Rosemary's attempt to decipher his meaning was rendered unnecessary when Eva made a tut-tut noise and said, "Surely you're not letting a silly thing like Friday the thirteenth get your wind up?"

"Well, no, I suppose not." Unconvincingly, Pembridge's cup and saucer rattled against one another. "But, well, one can't be too careful, can one? What's the harm in carrying a lucky charm, or avoiding walking under ladders, or—"

"Knocking on wood," Eva finished with evident amusement, rapping her knuckles against the wooden arm of her chair. "I suppose, if it makes you feel better, there's no harm at all. Though I must say, the English have rather tame superstitions compared to some places. In Prague, they have different ones entirely." She settled back with her own cup, clearly warming to the subject.

Finding the entire discussion rather silly, Rosemary maintained her polite expression and sipped her tea. Pembridge, meanwhile, nodded along earnestly, as though Eva were imparting the secrets of the universe rather than cataloging various forms of folkloric nonsense.

"My grandmother always said walking under ladders invites disaster. And never, ever open an umbrella indoors." He unconsciously twirled the rabbit's foot around on his finger as he spoke. Desdemona, having crept closer, watched the dangling charm with obvious fascination, tail flicking back and forth as if she might pounce at any moment.

"Ah yes, the umbrella!" Eva clapped her hands together. "Though I've always wondered about that one—surely the real danger is poking someone's eye out, not angering the household spirits? And did you know twins are considered bad luck in some cultures? Dreadful notion, really."

Rosemary grimaced, thinking of Vera, and the expression interrupted Eva's musings. "Did I say something wrong?"

"Not at all. It's just that my friend is due to give birth in a few short months," she explained, sparking a conversation regarding babies that might have continued indefinitely if Pembridge hadn't suddenly set down his teacup with purpose.

Eva came back to herself and began clearing stacks of books from the small table between them, revealing a leather portfolio beneath. "Well then, Mr. Pembridge, shall we attend to the business at hand? I've had a look at those Russian documents you brought, and I believe I can help."

Pembridge's nervous energy shifted into something more professional. "Mrs. Schweitzer, I cannot thank you enough. These old property records are giving me fits, and with the new assessments due..." He trailed off, casting an apologetic glance towards Rosemary. "I do hope you'll forgive my intrusion, Mrs. Lillywhite."

Mentally composing a polite excuse to leave, Rosemary waved off the apology while Eva explained, "Harold here is the tax assessor for the neighborhood. You can imagine how unwelcome that usually makes him."

Pembridge grimaced slightly. "Just doing my job, trying to be fair to everyone, but it's not often I'm invited in for tea."

"There's nothing to forgive," Rosemary assured politely, stowing her intention to excuse herself from the conversation and settling in for the duration.

"Actually," Pembridge clarified, "I work for the Historical Preservation Society in cooperation with the tax assessor's office. We identify architectural features of historical significance that must be preserved. I'm afraid it doesn't make me terribly popular. When I designate something as historically significant, the owners are legally required to maintain it to specific standards. The restoration work can be frightfully expensive, even when it doesn't affect the tax assessment itself."

"Oh dear," Rosemary murmured sympathetically. "I imagine that causes quite a bit of resentment."

"Rather." Pembridge attempted a weak smile, but his fingers worried at the rabbit's foot again. "I've been called everything from a 'meddling bureaucrat' to far less printable things. One gentleman threatened to have me sacked when I told him his crumbling garden wall was a listed feature from the 1740s."

"But surely people understand the importance of preserving history?" Rosemary asked, though she was already thinking of her own tax bill with mounting alarm.

"Not all of Marylebone is as posh as Park Road, and even so, you'd be surprised how quickly historical appreciation evaporates when faced with a restoration bill. The Ashfords had to delay their daughter's wedding when I informed them their Georgian windows couldn't be replaced with modern ones. They've not spoken to me since, and my daughter Emma's invitation to the event was rescinded. She still hasn't fully forgiven me," Pembridge said glumly.

Eva spread the documents across the now-cleared table, her reading glasses sliding down her nose as she examined the

Cyrillic script. "These date back over 150 years. Fascinating stuff, really—the original building specifications, architectural requirements from a property that had Russian owners."

"That's exactly what I'm hoping to preserve," Pembridge said, leaning forward with genuine enthusiasm. "I've been working my way through the neighborhood systematically, street by street, photographing all the architectural details before finalizing any assessments. Tonight I'm tackling the gargoyle over on Langford Street. It's an exceptional piece, and truly, it would be criminal to undervalue properties with such craftsmanship. I want to do right by these historic buildings. They deserve proper consideration."

As he spoke of preserving architectural details, Rosemary found her opinion of the anxious little man improving considerably.

"You know," Pembridge continued, his eyes brightening, "there are treasures hidden all over this city, behind facades and whatnot. Victorian modifications that were never properly documented, secret rooms, forgotten architectural details. I believe there's something secreted away at Mrs. Schmid's house, but when I tried to discuss it with her, we came a cropper. The proper wording for certain features does not always carry cleanly between our two languages. Her English is good, but my German is rubbish and the Swiss dialects only make the problem worse."

"Oh, the Swiss dialects are tricky," Eva agreed. "Even for native speakers, sometimes."

Rosemary had no idea if that was true or not. The neighborhood had a fair number of Swiss-German families, but she'd never given much thought to the linguistic complications they might face. Her own grasp of languages extended only to

French and a bit of Italian from holidays abroad. Eva, though, seemed comfortable with such things—the Russian documents on the table were proof enough of that.

Eva refilled their teacups with a gentle smile. "You're quite passionate about your work, Mr. Pembridge. Though I must say, you seem even more on edge than usual today."

Pembridge flinched at her observation, nearly spilling his tea. "Well, it's just been a rather trying week…"

"Come now," Eva said softly, her voice taking on the practiced tone of someone accustomed to coaxing confidences. "I've known you for weeks, and today you're practically jumping at shadows. What's troubling you?"

He clutched the rabbit's foot tighter, clearly conflicted about whether to continue in front of a stranger. "It's probably nothing. Just some unpleasant correspondence I've been receiving lately."

"What sort of correspondence?" Eva's voice sharpened with concern, and Rosemary's investigative instincts began to stir.

"Threats," Pembridge confirmed. "Anonymous ones, I'm afraid. Comes with the territory when you're reassessing people's taxes, but—" he cast an apologetic glance at Rosemary.

"Mr. Pembridge," she replied gently, "if it helps, I received threatening letters from the notorious murderer Garrison Black last year, so I'm rather scandal-proof at this point."

Both Eva and Pembridge stared at her with obvious surprise. His eyebrows rose in apparent reassessment, while her expression shifted to one of renewed fascination.

"Garrison Black?" Eva leaned forward with avid interest. "The rather twisted one who—"

"The very same," Rosemary confirmed. "So please, don't feel you need to spare my delicate sensibilities."

"I'd very much like to hear more about that later, but for now, Mr. Pembridge, you simply must show us these letters," Eva pressed.

"Oh, I couldn't possibly trouble you—"

"Nonsense!" Her tone brooked no argument. "You've come this far for help with the documents. A few nasty notes will hardly shock either of us."

Pembridge looked uncertainly between the two women, then sighed and reached into his jacket pocket, producing two folded pieces of paper with obvious reluctance. "They're probably nothing, really. Just someone letting off steam."

Eva unfolded the first letter and read aloud: "'Your luck won't last forever.'" She frowned and moved to the second. "'Those who meddle where they don't belong always get what's coming to them.'"

"Rather vague, aren't they?" Rosemary observed. "They're not demanding money or telling you to change a specific assessment. It sounds more like they simply want you to stop interfering—but with what?"

"Perhaps the writer doesn't want you discovering something," Eva suggested, studying the notes. "Or perhaps they want you out of the way entirely."

"In my profession," Pembridge said quietly, "I learn things. Sometimes they're things people don't want anyone to know." He knocked his knuckles against the wooden table automatically, the gesture so practiced it seemed unconscious.

Rosemary's attention sharpened at the dramatic phrasing. "Rather theatrical language," she mused aloud. "Not exactly the sort of thing one expects from a disgruntled homeowner."

"You know," Eva said thoughtfully, "the theater world is absolutely riddled with superstitions. They leave a light burning on stage at all times, and heaven help you if you whistle in the dressing room. It's all rather dramatic, really—much like these letters." She glanced at the threatening notes again. "Though I'm certain it's nothing to worry about. People who write angry letters rarely follow through."

Rosemary glanced at the small clock on Eva's mantelpiece and felt a jolt of alarm. "Goodness, I've completely lost track of time. I really must be getting on or I shall be late." She stood, gently displacing Dash from her lap.

"Perhaps I'll see you at the theater later, then," Eva said with a smile.

"That would be lovely," Rosemary replied.

As Pembridge stood to bid her goodbye, his pocket caught on the chair arm, sending his rabbit's foot and what appeared to be several other small charms scattering across the floor. He scrambled to collect them with obvious distress, muttering apologies under his breath.

Desdemona immediately pounced on the fallen rabbit's foot, batting at it playfully with her paws until Eva hurried over and gently shooed her away from the charm.

"Now then, you naughty thing, that's not a toy for you," Eva chided with amusement while helping Pembridge gather his belongings.

Rosemary knelt to help, noting the genuine fear in his eyes as he cataloged each recovered talisman. Whatever his reasons for such elaborate superstition, they ran deeper than mere quirk.

"Here," Eva pressed a small tin into Rosemary's hands. "Biscuits for your friend. And do bring Dash around again— he's made quite the impression."

Dash and Desdemona had apparently reached some sort of

understanding. The cat now sat washing her paws while keeping one lazy eye on the dog, and the earlier tension had dissolved into what could almost be called companionship.

The afternoon had taken an interesting turn. With her rapid topic changes and uncanny observations, Eva seemed odd at first, but there was a genuine kindness beneath the eccentricity. And Pembridge, for all his nervous energy and superstitious nonsense, clearly cared about preserving the neighborhood's architectural heritage.

Perhaps new neighbors weren't such a bad thing after all, Rosemary mused.

"Auf Wiedersehen," Eva called cheerfully as Rosemary made her way to the door.

"Auf Veeder—Vieder—" Pembridge attempted valiantly before giving up with a rueful shake of his head. "Goodbye, Mrs. Lillywhite."

On the footway outside Eva's front door, a man walked past who could have been another of the Redberrys' workers—built like a brick house and wearing a similar uniform—though he wore a flat cap pulled low and had a noticeable limp in his left leg.

Dash launched into another round of barking. Here we go again, Rosemary thought wearily, but the man barked out a sharp command in German—"Schweigen!"—and to her amazement, Dash immediately fell silent and sat back on his haunches.

Rosemary froze as well. A German command barked at that volume carried a particular echo for anyone who'd lived through the war. The moment passed quickly, but it left her distinctly unsettled.

The man gave her a friendly nod and continued on his way, whistling cheerfully. Perfectly harmless, of course. Rosemary tried to commit the command to memory—something beginning with S—though she wasn't entirely certain she'd be able to reproduce it. Still, it might prove useful the next time Dash decided to serenade the entire neighborhood.

A Case of Luck and Death is available now. Keep reading for a preview of the free novella you'll get for joining my newsletter.

Enjoyed meeting Rosemary? Not ready for her story to end? If you sign up for my newsletter, you will receive The Case of the Misdelivered Valentine, a novella featuring Rosemary Lillywhite as my gift for hanging out with me.

When love is at stake, Rosemary is on the case!
In this prequel to The Case at Barton Manor, Rosemary Lillywhite solves her first case. When Rosemary receives an unexpected gift on Valentine's day, a gift that was not meant for her, she sets out to solve the mystery of the mistaken delivery.

Excerpt from The Case of the Misdelivered Valentine

Rosemary Lillywhite, draped across her settee in a deceptively languid pose, put her glass down on the end table and stubbed out the cigarette from which she had taken a single drag. The taste of tobacco coated her mouth, and she scrunched her nose in distaste. The scent was what reminded her of Andrew, anyway, and the positively acrid taste had done nothing to improve her mental state.

Rosemary had been dreading Valentine's Day ever since her maudlin mood ruined Christmas and turned New Year's Eve into a personal pity party rather than a celebration of new beginnings. Thankfully, this holiday would not inspire a spate of invitations to be regretfully declined.

Enduring such events as a widow brought on sympathetic stares from everyone who knew she'd lost her husband, not to mention platitudes offered by well-wishers who didn't understand how their condolences only made her plight all the more vivid. Instead of soothing the passing of time and the pain of growing older without the man with whom she'd expected to experience all the gifts life had to offer, their comments made barricading herself at home and avoiding all contact with the outside world a much more enticing prospect.

Valentine's Day, above all others, inspired within her a dread she could not ignore. Each year of her five with Andrew, Rosemary's front table bloomed with a big bouquet of beautiful roses—red for love, of course—tokens from her doting husband to exemplify how much she was adored. This year, there would be no roses, save for the white ones she'd draped across his headstone. White for purity, white for remembrance.

Rosemary sighed and took up the glass again to consider the inch of gin. Roses to remember, alcohol to forget. She raised the drink to her lips, then set it down with a click and another sigh as a thumping sound echoed from the front entrance through the nearby door to the parlor where she was unhappily ensconced.

"Bother," she muttered, and a moment later, she heard a familiar voice muffled by the wavy glass.

"Rosie, open up, I say." More knocking. "Where are you?"

Rather than answer, Rosemary closed her eyes and vehemently hoped her friend would just go away—a fanciful wish, as giving up simply wasn't in Vera's repertoire.

A few seconds later, the last remnants of her wish disappeared as quickly as the tendrils of smoke from the cigarette, as Vera threw open the parlor door and squinted into the darkness.

"If you wanted to keep me out, you should not have given me a spare key." Vera said, brandishing the offending object, then tucked it carefully into her clutch. The rolling of her eyes annoyed Rosemary, who now huddled on the settee, her hair a wild mess around her face and her eyes red-rimmed from crying.

"A mistake I intend to rectify the moment my vision returns." Rosemary threw an arm up over her eyes when the drapes rattled open to let in the sun. "I suppose there's little use in asking you to leave me to my misery."

"None whatsoever." Cheerful and determined, Vera whirled around the room setting things to rights and making Rosemary tired by the simple fact of her animated presence. "You simply must stop moping, dear one," she chided.

"You're a tiresome bother to me." Yet, Rosemary was touched by the effort on her emotional behalf, and found it straining to maintain a morose manner when Vera finally plunked down upon the opposite end of the settee. "Why can't you let me have a good wallow and drown my sorrows in peace?"

Vera waved off the plea. "Where on earth is the staff? Your Wadsworth usually doesn't miss a beat, certainly not a knock at the door. The state of this room is an absolute disgrace."

"I gave them all the day off. It is a holiday, after all, and they should all be allowed to spend it with their own loved ones," Rosemary replied, her voice dull and monotone. It hadn't been easy to convince her butler or her personal maid, Anna, to leave her alone in the house, but neither the cook nor the house-keeper had protested overmuch.

"Why, it's barely noon. You mean to say this is the result of a single morning without help? What would the place look like in a week?"

The nerve of the woman, Rosemary thought, and then said in a dry tone, "Are you calling me a slob, darling? Or saying I have excellent taste in staff? I can hardly tell the difference."

There must still be a little fire left in her if she could participate in verbal volley. "Yes, well, had you insisted they stay on, you might have received news of this bouquet of roses before the blooms drowned on your front stoop." Vera reprimanded Rosemary as gently as she was able.

Rosemary pulled her arm down to really look at Vera for the first time, and saw her friend burying a pert nose in a riot of blood-red roses Her heart lurching, Rosemary felt a burst of hope as if perhaps Andrew's death and the long months alone might be nothing more than a fevered dream.

Vera set the crystal vase full of flowers down on the coffee table in front of Rosemary and handed her friend the card that had been tucked among the fragrant petals. Unable to bring herself to open the card, Rosemary merely stared at it, turning it over in her hands while fresh tears welled in her eyes. "Who on earth could have sent them?" She asked aloud.

"There's only one way to find out." Vera reached over and took the card, carefully opening it and reading aloud:

'My dearest Betty,

I still love you after all these years. My heart is filled with regret, and I wish I had been brave enough to fight for you as I should have done.

If you still feel the same way, meet me at our special place in time to watch the sunset.

I hope it's not too late, and that you'll be my Valentine today and every day forward.

Love,

JLH'

"Well," Vera breathed, "They definitely aren't for you. I wonder if they were meant for one of your neighbors."

Even in her melancholy state, Rosemary was touched by the message written on the card, and her mind raced through the names of the people who lived on her block. "There isn't a

Betty on this street, I'm sure of it. Perhaps the florist made a mistake, and these flowers were supposed to go to one of the other London boroughs."

"It's possible. Why don't we call round and ask who sent them, and to what address. It would be a pity if they never reached their intended destination." Vera strode back out to the front hall where the telephone was located and beckoned for her friend to follow.

She waited for the operator to connect her to the Gold Crown Flower Shop, then explained the situation. "All right. I understand." Vera said, and hung up. "This is the intended address. The shop girl also said there was no contact information given with the order. The fellow who made the order seemed nervous, and stressed clearly that the flowers were to go to Number 8, Park Road."

"Well," Rosemary said, "The card did say *after all these years*, and we've only owned this house for the last five."

"So the gift might have been meant for some prior occupant?" Vera deduced.

Rosemary nodded, "Yes, but you must remember, this building contained a series of flats when we purchased it. We spent a simply ghastly year turning it into a townhouse. It could have been any one of those tenants. Oh—" She jumped up, the dressing gown she'd worn all day billowing around her waist.

"What is it?" Vera asked.

The Case of the Misdelivered Valentine is only available by signing up for my newsletter. Keep reading for an explanation of the British English terms and slang used in the book!